THE FORTUNES OF TEXAS

*Follow the lives and loves of a complex family
with a rich history and deep ties
in the Lone Star State*

FORTUNE'S FAMILY SECRETS

With Archibald Fortune's death comes the revelation of a stunning secret: The Emerald Ridge scion had three separate families and one child he'd always longed to find! Can his shocked children come together to find Archibald's missing heir and claim the family inheritance—or will strife tear them apart?

FORTUNE'S SURPRISE REUNION

After an accident upends her life, superstar actress Susannah Simmons retreats to idyllic Emerald Ridge for comfort. Rekindling romance with a love from years before—a love who's just discovered he's part of the Fortune dynasty— was not in her plans! But sometimes, life's winding road is full of surprises...

Dear Reader,

Welcome back to Emerald Ridge and the world of the iconic Fortunes of Texas!

I'm thrilled to be a part of this legendary romance series. I always love spending time with this dramatic and glamorous family, where the characters and plots are Texas-sized and larger than life. I was especially excited to write this particular book, because it's the conclusion of the latest Fortunes miniseries called Fortune's Family Secrets. And guess what, y'all? This miniseries celebrates the thirtieth anniversary of the Fortunes of Texas!

This book is also its own romance story, of course, so get ready to meet Oliver and Susannah. Their romance is a twist on the classic *Beauty and the Beast*, one of my favorite fairy tales. This story and the entire miniseries are full of dramatic twists and turns. Be sure to pick up the first five books in Fortune's Family Secrets to get the full effect of everything happening with our favorite Texan dynasty. You can find them at Harlequin.com or any online retailer.

I hope you enjoy your literary trip to this fun Texas town. As always, thank you for reading!

XOXO,

Teri

FORTUNE'S SURPRISE REUNION

TERI WILSON

THE FORTUNES OF TEXAS

Special thanks and acknowledgment are given to Teri Wilson for her contribution to The Fortunes of Texas: Fortune's Family Secrets miniseries.

THE FORTUNES
OF TEXAS

Recycling programs for this product may not exist in your area.

ISBN-13: 978-1-335-14336-5

Fortune's Surprise Reunion

Harlequin Enterprises ULC
22 Adelaide St. West, 41st Floor
Toronto, Ontario M5H 4E3, Canada
www.Harlequin.com

HarperCollins Publishers
Macken House, 39/40 Mayor Street Upper,
Dublin 1, D01 C9W8, Ireland
www.HarperCollins.com

Printed in Lithuania

1 2 3 4 5 6 7 8 9 10 LIT 28 27 26 25

New York Times bestselling author **Teri Wilson** writes heartwarming, feel-good contemporary romance with a touch of whimsy. Four of Teri's books have been adapted into Hallmark Channel movies, including fan favorite *Unleashing Mr. Darcy*. Teri is a recipient of the prestigious RITA® Award for Excellence in Romantic Fiction and a recent inductee into the San Antonio Women's Hall of Fame. When not writing, Teri enjoys spreading doggy joy with her Cavalier King Charles spaniel, Charm, a registered therapy dog.

Books by Teri Wilson

The Fortunes of Texas: Fortune's Family Secrets

Fortune's Surprise Reunion

The Fortunes of Texas: Secrets of Fortune's Gold Ranch

A Fortune's Secret

Harlequin Special Edition

Texas Forever After

The Perfect Pass

Comfort Paws

Dog Days of Summer
Fa-La-La-La Faking It
Bluebonnet Season

Love, Unveiled

Her Man of Honor
Faking a Fairy Tale

Visit the Author Profile page
at Harlequin.com for more titles.

To the enduring spirit of Camp Mystic,
where generations have found friendship,
faith and joy beneath the Texas skies.

XOXO

Chapter One

Susannah Simmons cracked one eye open before dawn could fully break, the gentle sound of paws tip-tapping on wood her unofficial alarm clock. In the months since she'd adopted her trio of Labrador retrievers from a Texas breed rescue, she hadn't slept past six thirty in the morning. They kept her on a tight schedule, never letting her forget when it was time for breakfast, dinner or a walk. She'd never realized that dogs had such remarkable internal clocks, like they could feel the minutes ticking away in their bones.

Honestly, Susannah didn't mind it one bit. She'd spent enough of the past year wallowing in bed. It was nice to have a reason to get up in the morning again…

Even if that reason was a wet nose pressed to her cheek at precisely 6:29, followed by a second one burrowing its way under her covers and a third nudging her hand, angling for pats despite her semiconscious state.

"Good morning, guys," she murmured, sleep clinging to her voice.

Hershey's tail thumped once against the polished oak floor. Honey let out a subdued huff. Bear simply sat near the foot of the bed, vigilant and still as a statue.

They were a perfect set, one in each color—chocolate, yellow and black, like someone had checked a box for every shade of Labrador. Susannah had originally intended on adopting only one of them, but the moment she'd seen them sharing an exercise pen together at their foster home, her plan had gone straight out the window.

Granted, three big dogs had seemed like a lot, but Susannah had plenty of time on her hands now to devote to their care. This was what starting over was supposed to be about, right? Reinventing yourself in a major way. She no longer needed to worry about memorizing lines, long shoots on location or attending a different A-list event every night in the Hollywood Hills. Susannah had wanted a dog her entire life, but it hadn't seemed fair to add a pet to the mix when her life was such a whirlwind.

That wasn't an issue anymore. *At all.* If Labs had come in a fourth color, she might've gone all in on a quartet.

With a groan muffled by the warm quilt, she swung her legs over the side of the bed and flexed her ankle. A dull ache radiated up her calf as she stood, her limp automatic now, the pain a quiet companion instead of a foe. The big log house, all warm pine and exposed beams, stretched quietly around her. It was luxurious in a rustic Texas way but softened with piles of dog beds and patchwork quilts.

She caught her reflection in the window glass as she passed. Even blurred by morning condensation, the scar across her left cheek flared white against her skin. Her breath hitched—just for a moment. It always did. Then she looked away.

The kitchen was airy with soft, golden light filtering through the delicate lace curtains. Her house in California had been outfitted with blackout window coverings to afford a sliver of privacy. Paparazzi weren't too much of a concern in Emerald Ridge, Texas, though. The media had just about given up on circling the property to try and find out why she'd shunned the spotlight. Every now and then, she heard about a journalist or two showing up in town and asking questions, but the last sighting had been months ago. No one was using a long lens to try and catch a glimpse of her anymore. Her star had well and truly fallen.

She padded around the kitchen in her sock feet, scooping kibble, pouring fresh water and flipping the switch on the coffee maker. Bear poked his muzzle into her hip as she moved. Honey circled like a yellow whirlwind. And Hershey... He wagged with unwavering loyalty. They didn't see the scar. Or maybe they did and simply didn't care—just one of the reasons dogs were so amazing. Better than people, for the most part.

Certainly better than Brett.

Her hands tightened around her ceramic mug. Steam curled up from the coffee in a fragrant ribbon, and she closed her eyes as she took her first sip. Then she lifted her fingertips and absently brushed them against the ridge of her scar, a habit she hated but couldn't seem to break. Her cheek still felt foreign, even after all this time.

"You've changed too much," Brett had said.

Too much for her career. Too much for their future. Too much, period.

Her jaw tightened. The memory always came with the smell of antiseptic and Juliet roses, reminiscent of the hospital and the overly lavish bouquet he'd brought the day he walked away.

Susannah much preferred the wildflowers that grew in thick bunches around the walking path that snaked through the woods on her property here in Emerald Ridge. There was something special about colorful blooms that thrived all on their own, without being pruned or fawned over. Maybe she'd pick a few today and arrange them in a Mason jar on the kitchen island.

A bark broke her reverie, and she jumped. Honey stared at her with those soulful eyes that saw too much. Susannah forced a smile and knelt, letting her pups crowd her, press their noses into her hands and their flanks against her legs. They were the reason she was still here—on this land, in this remote house, in her own skin.

"Okay, okay. I can take a hint," she said, and their tails whipped back and forth. "Time for our morning walk."

She slipped her feet into the plain white sneakers that sat by the kitchen door and grabbed her walking stick—a rustic length of twisted hickory she'd bought from the gift shop at the nearby Fortune's Gold Ranch and Spa. As the dogs danced in place, nails clicking against the hardwood, she reached for the hoodie she always wore on her rare trips into town. Her shield. Then she thought better of it. She didn't need it here on her estate, and she still wasn't quite accustomed to the scorching Texas summer heat. Even at this time of day, her simple eyelet top and faded jeans would be plenty warm.

She opened the door and followed her dogs into the damp morning air, the scent of pine and rich earth welcoming them to the peaceful world of Emerald Ridge. Mist clung to the trees, the grass was tipped with dew drops and, aside from the mourning doves and mockingbirds that Texas was so famous for, all was quiet. It had taken Susannah months to stop listening for the telltale sound of a camera shutter every time she walked outside. She'd finally grown used to the blessed silence.

Hershey, Honey and Bear scampered ahead of her, sniffing the earthy ground. Susannah leaned on her walking stick as she followed, placing one foot carefully after the other, each step its own small victory. The hiking trail that wound like a ribbon through the trees was her favorite thing about her sprawling new property. Her ranch was so big that she could walk for hours without ever leaving her own little slice of heaven or bumping into another person.

Or so she'd thought…

Bear was the first to notice that something was off. His ears pricked forward as he lifted his head, eyes focused intently on the horizon. Even then, Susannah wasn't alarmed. She figured the black Lab had just spotted a squirrel. The forest was full of them, and in the mornings, they liked to chase each other from limb to limb, scrambling up and down the thick trunks of the pecan trees. But then Honey let out a sharp bark. In a flash, all three dogs took off and disappeared around a bend in the trail.

Susannah froze, fingertips curling around twisted hickory. Her dogs never ran ahead of her like that. Panic coiled low in her belly, and she tried to tell herself it was probably nothing. They were canines, after all. They'd probably spotted a fox or one of the white-tailed deer that liked to graze in the lower pasture.

But then a chorus of barks broke through the silence, and she forced herself forward, digging her stick into the ground with each step.

"Easy," she called, not sure whether she was speaking to her dogs or herself. "Stay close."

She was almost to the bend when she heard it—the unmistakable crunch of footsteps on the path. Her breath caught in her throat. Someone was on her land.

"Hershey!" she yelled. "Honey! Bear!"

She gave the *come* command, praying they would scamper back to her side with their tails wagging and tongues lolling out of the sides of their mouths. But they didn't. Instead, a fresh round of excited barks rang out. The sort of barks reserved for tennis balls, treats or making new friends.

Of course. Labs were sweetness personified—loving, loyal and absolutely useless as guard dogs. So useless, in fact, that Susannah had invested in an audio decoy security feature as part of her home's alarm system. Whenever someone set foot on her property, a recording of ferocious barking blasted through hidden outdoor speakers. Instant Rottweiler energy, courtesy of modern technology.

Now, Susannah wanted nothing more than to flee back to her fortress, but she couldn't leave her real-life, lovable dogs. What was she going to do? She wasn't ready for this. Who would be trespassing on her property, anyway? Surely not a reporter.

Why, oh *why*, hadn't she gone ahead and shrugged into her hoodie?

She took a deep breath and rounded the bend, heart hammering in her chest. The wind lifted her hair just enough to expose the edge of her cheek. She reached up instinctively to cover it, but she was too late. There they all were, all three of her dogs clustered around a stranger like he'd just offered them bacon and a ride to the riverbank.

She swallowed hard and regarded the man for a beat before hastily covering her face with her hair. He was tall and muscular, with dark hair and soft brown eyes. Like a lot of the other men here in Texas, he wore a Stetson, but there was something different about him. Something almost…familiar?

"Sorry," he said, his voice low and warm. "I didn't mean to cause a commotion. I think I just made three new friends."

He held his hands up as the dogs circled him, wagging their entire back ends and sniffing him like he was already part of the pack. *Her* pack.

She needed to get the dogs and get back to the house. The man seemed friendly enough, and he appeared to be a local, not someone on the hunt for a famous actress who'd vanished from the spotlight overnight. But he was still a stranger. And Susannah didn't like to be around people anymore. Not even people her dogs seemed to have developed an instant crush on.

She gave the man a polite but firm nod. "This is private property. The trail ends at the gate."

"Right, I'm sorry. I—" he started, then his dark eyes glittered beneath the rim of his cowboy hat as his gaze lingered on her face. Not in that startled, pitying way that most people looked at her scar, but with something else.

Recognition.

"Suzy?" he said, the name gentle and familiar, as if it still belonged to her after all these years. "Suzy Simmons?"

Oliver Fortune Dunhill couldn't believe his eyes.

He would've recognized Susannah Simmons anywhere. She was famous, after all. Not regular famous, like an actress from a television sitcom or one of the country-western stars who played at the big Texas rodeos or the Grand Ole Opry. *Big-time* famous. Susannah Simmons was a legit movie star—the kind who sat front row at the Oscars and couldn't venture out in public without being surrounded by bodyguards.

He glanced around, half expecting a former navy SEAL to jump out from behind a tree and tackle him to the ground for speaking to her. Was he really trespassing? He hadn't spent enough time yet on his newly inherited patch of land in Emerald Ridge to recognize the property lines by sight. If he'd crossed an invisible boundary line and ended up on her side of the woods, Oliver should probably be grateful no one had taken a shot at him yet. She didn't seem to have protection here in Texas, though. The trio of Labradors hardly counted, unless they planned on licking him to death.

"Oren?" She blinked at him and gasped as a slow smile tipped her lips—lips that he remembered well. They'd been soft and hesitant the first time they'd touched his, tasting faintly of cherry lip gloss and tart summer limeade. "Is it really you?"

He stammered for a beat, unsure how to answer. "Yes…and no."

That was about as clear as mud. No wonder her smile faltered, brows drawing together in confusion.

"It's really me. I promise." He gave a dry chuckle. "I just don't go by Oren anymore."

He didn't go by Dunn anymore, either. In the ten-plus years since he and Susannah had stolen a kiss in the cool, blue-green water of Austin's Barton Creek, where they met while on vacation with their respective families, Oliver's name had changed enough times that his friends had begun to crack jokes about the witness protection program. For the record, he wasn't in witness protection…that he knew of, anyway. But all his life, Oliver had wondered who he really was and where he came from.

He'd always had a great relationship with his mom, Lorna Dunn. May she rest in peace, but she'd kept her secrets close to her chest. Secrets like who Oliver's father was and why, on his eighteenth birthday, she'd asked him to change his name from Oren Dunn to Oliver Webb. She'd already been sick by then, and he hadn't wanted to cause her any more pain or stress, so he'd acquiesced and accepted the new driver's license, passport and other official-looking documents she'd presented to him, no questions asked. Growing up, he'd come to realize his mother had money—the sort of money that could buy things like new identities. She'd changed her name from Lorna Dunn to Lesley Webb at the same time she'd begged him to become Oliver Webb.

Why, though? That was the question that had kept him awake at night in the years that followed. After his mom passed away a decade ago, he'd tried to forget all the unanswered questions and honor her memory by not poking into her past. He'd pressed so many times over the years and she'd always refused to talk about it. Maybe some secrets were meant to remain gone and buried with their keepers.

But the truth had a way of eating away at a person, and as the decade since his mother's passing wore on, Oliver had grown increasingly anxious. Earlier this year, he'd packed up and moved to Emerald Ridge from his ranch near Austin, hoping to learn something about his mother's past since the small Texas resort town was where she'd been born. Discovering his father's identity had been right at the top of the list, but nothing could've prepared Oliver for the truth.

"My name is Oliver now," he said, as if a simple name switcheroo could explain everything that had transpired since he'd relocated to Emerald Ridge. In a matter of months, his life had become a soap opera.

He wondered when, and *if*, his head would ever stop spinning. "It's kind of a long story."

Understatement of the century, he thought as she regarded him with unabashed curiosity. A gentle breeze lifted her lush blond hair, and his breath caught as he glimpsed a scar on the side of her face—jagged, pale and wholly unexpected.

He willed himself not to react. Not to flinch. Not to let his gaze linger. Something about the way she'd first responded to a stranger on her property had struck him as unlike the free-spirited girl he used to know. Maybe the scar and the walking stick she gripped in her right hand had something to do with it. Whatever the cause, she was every bit as beautiful as she'd been that sun-drenched summer all those years ago. More so, if such a thing was even possible.

"A long story?" She tilted her head, and at the sound of her voice, the three rambunctious Labradors trotted away from him and sat at her feet, gazing up at her like she was their sun, moon and stars, all wrapped up into one. "I've got time on my hands."

Something deep in Oliver's chest stirred—slow, aching and strange. Like the years between them had thinned in an instant, slipping through his fingers the moment she looked at him like that, with the same quiet attentiveness he remembered from the days they used to talk until dusk.

He took a breath, steadying himself. This was *Susannah Simmons*, for crying out loud. She was probably just being nice to an old acquaintance she barely remembered. They'd been just fourteen years old back then. She'd been his very first kiss. But a lot had changed since those sparkling summer days. Oliver didn't keep up with celebrity gossip, but he hadn't been living under a rock. Every time he went through the grocery store checkout, he spotted Susannah on the cover of a magazine. More often than not, she'd been pictured at some glamorous Hollywood event with an A-list actor on her arm.

He still didn't even know what she was doing here. He'd heard she'd moved to Emerald Ridge, and social media gossip had mentioned an accident, but details were scarce and, half the time, unreliable. Was she filming a movie nearby?

Could she possibly own the sprawling ranch directly next door to the land he'd recently inherited? She'd all but accused him of trespassing just now. What were the odds?

Not that it mattered much. When Oliver had known her, he'd been a shy boy with a bad haircut who once picked her daisies from the park next to the springs and shared his last watermelon Popsicle. He highly doubted she remembered much more than his name.

Still, her words snagged in his head like a loose thread he couldn't stop pulling at.

I've got time on my hands...

"You really mean that?" he asked.

"Yes. I haven't spent much time around people lately, and it might be nice to catch up with an old friend," she said.

Just as he suspected. She remembered his name, but he doubted she remembered much else.

Susannah's smile softened as her fingers curled absently in the fur of the Lab closest to her—the chocolate-brown one. The dog panted as it gazed at Oliver, its mouth stretched into a big doggy grin. If these animals were supposed to be bodyguards, she had good reason to be concerned for her safety.

"I'd like that," he said, clearing his throat.

He took a tentative step closer, hands tucked into the pockets of his Wranglers, not quite sure what to say next.

Susannah tilted her head again, studying him with a warmth in her gaze that made the years between them blur just a little bit more. He almost believed he caught a glimmer of their shared past still quietly alive in her eyes. "Any chance you still like limeade, Oren…or Oliver…or whoever you are now?"

He huffed a laugh. "Oliver's fine. And yeah, I still like limeade."

She grinned and gestured for him to follow her. Then she led the way down the wooded trail with her dogs trotting faithfully on her heels. Oliver kept step behind them, drawn by the quiet, impossible truth…

Susannah Simmons remembered him, after all.

Chapter Two

Susannah squeezed another lime with her citrus juicer while sugar dissolved in a saucepan on the stove. Her hands shook slightly every time she remembered that Oliver stood just a few feet away as she moved through the simple task, the motion feeling suddenly clumsy under his quiet gaze. She'd forgotten what it was like to have an audience.

"Do you do this often?" Oliver quirked an eyebrow. "Whip up your own homemade limeade?"

"Never, actually," she said as she added the lime juice to the mixture on the stove and gave it a stir with her favorite wooden spoon. "I was planning on making a key lime pie, so I happen to have a bunch of limes on hand. I'm a bit new to all this."

"New to limes?" Oliver leaned against the counter, watching her with a mixture of curiosity and amusement. "Or citrus fruit, in general?"

Susannah wasn't sure what had prompted her to invite him inside her home. The words had come tumbling out of her mouth before she could stop them. Scratch that—she knew where the sudden invitation had come from. She just didn't *want* to admit it. Not even to herself.

The truth was, after purposefully planning her new life to avoid any and all human contact, Susannah was a tiny bit lonely. She loved her solitary life on her ranch, but every now and then, she missed the comfort of casual conversation.

She hadn't expected to miss people. For weeks, she'd been perfectly content with only herself and her dogs for company. The very idea of venturing into town without her disguise was horrifying. After the way Brett had treated her while she was recovering in the hospital, she just couldn't take it. If someone who'd professed to love her had been so shaken by the change in her appearance, how would the general public react?

The thought terrified her. So she'd hidden herself away, and until Oliver had appeared on her land out of nowhere, like a time traveler from sweet summer days when everything brimmed with innocence and hope, she hadn't realized how lonesome she'd become.

Oliver was different, though. So different, in fact, that she kept forgetting to hide her face behind her curtain of tousled blond hair. With him, she almost felt like her old self—not the perfect Hollywood princess, but the simple girl who'd loved doing cannonballs and eating sun-ripened strawberries straight from the vine.

Like Suzy, not Susannah.

Oliver had known her before she became famous. Before the movies or red carpets. Way, *way* before *People* magazine put her on the cover of their Most Beautiful issue…*twice*. With him, she could almost pretend that entire period of her life had never really happened.

"New to limes? Really?" A warm hum of mirth slipped past her lips. When was the last time someone had made her laugh? "More like new to domesticity."

A few months ago, the thought of making home-made anything would've never crossed Susannah's mind. When she'd moved into her log fortress tucked into the woods, she hadn't even known how to turn on the stove. Why would she? Back in California, she'd had a whole staff of people to do things for her.

But *starting over* meant learning new things. Other than her dogs, she was utterly alone in this house. In the beginning, finding her way around a kitchen had been a necessity. Once she got used to it, she'd realized she enjoyed preparing her own meals. Soon, she began spending long hours at the big butcher block island, toying with new recipes while Hershey, Honey and Bear sprawled on the patchwork dog beds scattered about the floor. Now that she'd abandoned the calorie-tracking app her personal trainer back in California had demanded that she use, she especially enjoyed making desserts. Hence, the overflowing fruit bowl of limes, just begging to become a pie.

Oliver snagged one of the plump green limes, tossed it into the air, then caught it and handed it to her. "I'm not sure I believe you're new to this. You're moving around this kitchen like a pro."

"I'm an actress, remember? This is all an illusion. Also, you should've seen me when I first moved here. On my very first night, I made frozen pizza for dinner and accidentally cooked it with the cardboard backing still attached."

"No biggie. I think we've all made that mistake once or twice." Oliver winked at her, but she thought she spied a twitch at the corner of his lips like he was trying not to laugh. "How long have you lived in Emerald Ridge?"

Susannah shrugged one shoulder as she stirred the mixture on the stove. "About six months now, I guess."

"So this isn't just a break or a vacation, then? It's permanent?" he asked, and she wondered if the hopefulness she heard in his tone was real or imagined.

Stop blushing like an idiot. He's just being nice.

She forced a smile but kept her gaze glued to the stove. "Definitely permanent. I was in a bad car accident a while back, and it officially put an end to my acting career. No one wants to see me on-screen anymore."

"I doubt that's true," he said with a tenderness that made her throat clog. "I can think of one person who'd love to see you anywhere."

Oliver came closer, lifted his fingertips, and for a panicked second, Susannah thought he might brush the hair from her face and force her to meet his gaze. She nearly forgot how to breathe. But then Hershey scrambled to his feet and nudged his way between them, the big goofball. Her hero, right on cue. The chocolate Lab had just earned himself an extra scoop of kibble with his dinner later tonight.

"Enough about me. You still haven't told me why you're here in Emerald Ridge and what this name-change business is all about," she said brightly—*too* brightly, probably. If Oliver noticed, he was kind enough to pretend otherwise.

"My mom was born here in Emerald Ridge," he said, and his smile turned bittersweet around the edges. "She passed away a little more than ten years ago."

Susannah pressed a hand to her heart. "I'm so sorry. That must've been really difficult for you."

When they'd met as kids, Oliver had been on vacation with his mother—no one else, just her. She was the only family he had. Ten years ago, he would've been barely eighteen or nineteen. Susannah couldn't imagine losing your only parent at such a young age.

"It was pretty rough for a while. I loved my mother—you know that. But she was a closed book, and she seemed to get even more secretive after she got sick," he said, emotion flickering just beneath the surface.

"How so?" Susannah asked. Why did she get the feeling that his mother's death was just the tip of the iceberg?

"For starters, for my eighteenth birthday, her gift to me was an entirely new identity. New name, new government documents, the whole shebang. That's when I became Oliver Webb instead of Oren Dunn."

Susannah blinked. "Did she say why?"

Oliver shook his head. "No, she refused to talk about it. But she insisted I go along with the change and I just needed to trust her. Mom said something about a new slate, but I knew something wasn't right. She was already so sick then, though. I didn't want to cause her any undue stress, so I did as she asked."

"You're a good son, Oliver." Susannah wasn't sure she could've done the same. Then again, she and her mom hadn't really been close. Her mother had always had a flair for the dramatic, poking her nose into everyone else's business and stirring the pot. She'd feuded with more members of Susannah's family than she could count.

Oliver removed his Stetson to run a hand through his thick, dark hair and then replaced it as he blew out a breath. "I'm not sure Mom would agree. I tried to honor her wishes and let the past stay buried like she wanted, but eventually I just had to know where I came from, who my father was and why everything was so wrapped up in secrecy. It was really starting to nag at me. With Mom gone, I couldn't really let it go."

"So here you are," Susannah said, and she couldn't help but smile. No matter how he'd ended up on her little slice of Lone Star paradise, she was glad he was here.

"So here I am." His eyes glittered like he was glad, too.

Hershey, ever her protector, let out a huff. He was acting like the flirt police, which was a good thing. Susannah needed a friend, not romance. Her heart was far too tender to even think about something more.

She broke his gaze, and her pulse fluttered like a butterfly caught in a net as she poured the limeade mixture into a pitcher filled with ice and thinly sliced limes. "Tell me the rest. Did you find the answers you were looking for?"

She hoped so. Everyone deserved to know who they

really were. In a way, Susannah was on a similar path of discovery. Without her career, and without the face and body that had made her famous, who *was* she?

"I did. It's been a wild ride, but I know exactly who I am now. My full name is Oliver Fortune Dunhill, and I just inherited the parcel of land next door." He flashed her a lopsided smile, and for a split second, he looked just like the boy she used to know—mischief in his eyes and hope in his grin. "Howdy, neighbor."

"Did you say…" Susannah swallowed hard, loud enough for Oliver to hear "…*neighbor*?"

He'd sort of hoped for a more positive reaction, or at least one that didn't make her look like she'd just seen a ghost in cowboy boots.

She's just a little skittish, that's all, Oliver told himself. It didn't take a genius to figure out she was self-conscious about her appearance. He wondered how often she ventured off her property. Never, from the sound of things. If she'd been spotted in town even once, word would've spread like wildfire.

"I did indeed." He nodded, injecting as much casual ease into his voice as he could, even though his heart was galloping double time. He wasn't about to say it out loud—not yet—but a tiny part of him couldn't help wondering if maybe this was fate. He just hoped she didn't bolt before he had a chance to find out.

"That's quite a coincidence." Her tone was neutral, but Oliver didn't miss the way her eyes flickered toward the window like she was already calculating an escape route. Then she blinked, and her gaze swiveled his direction again. "Wait a minute. Your name is Fortune now? As in, *the* Fortunes?"

"Yep, *those* Fortunes," he said. The family was iconic, with Texas roots that went back generations. Susannah didn't know the half of it yet, though. Oliver could barely wrap his head around it himself. "My dad was Archibald Fortune, founder of Fortune Air. I just got the results back from the DNA test a month or so ago. Unfortunately, he died suddenly earlier this year, so I never got the chance to know him."

"It must have been heartbreaking to find out who he was, only to learn he'd recently passed away." Susannah sat down on the barstool closest to him and pushed a chilled jar full of limeade toward him across the kitchen island. Her fingertips lingered on the butcher block, just a whisper away from his.

She felt it too, didn't she…this strange temptation to fall right back into the past?

Oliver's breath seemed to bottle up tight in his chest. Then, just as he convinced himself he wasn't imagining the invisible thread stretching between them, pulling them back to the warm summer sunshine of yesterday, she pulled her hand back. Her fingers wrapped around her jar of limeade until her knuckles turned white.

He cleared his throat, reminding himself who the woman sitting beside him really was—Susannah Simmons, one of the most famous women on the planet. Not his sweet Suzy who'd danced barefoot in the grass and splashed in the springs like she didn't have a care in the world. The accident had clearly rattled her, but surely she wasn't planning on hiding out in Emerald Ridge forever.

"I guess you could say it was heartbreaking," he admitted, although he hadn't felt that way at first. In the beginning, he hadn't wanted any part of the Fortunes. It had taken five siblings he hadn't even known he had to change his mind. "Like everything else about my past, it was also complicated. As it turns out, during the time my mother and Archibald were involved, he was married…"

Susannah's eyes widened over the rim of her glass as she sipped her drink.

"…to three different women."

She choked on her limeade. *"Three?"* she croaked, setting the jar down with a soft thud. "As in, simultaneously?"

Oliver gave a short, humorless laugh. "Yep. My mom only knew about one of them at first—Agatha. She was the only one from Emerald Ridge."

Susannah's brows arched, and her vibrant green eyes held his for a beat too long. "So Lorna and Agatha knew each other?"

He tilted his head. "Sort of, although my mom's name was Lianna back then. She didn't know the full story, though—not right away. Once she found out she was pregnant with me, she gave Archibald an ultimatum. Leave Agatha or…"

He trailed off, jaw flexing with restrained emotion. His mother wasn't perfect. She'd made her share of mistakes, but no woman should have to deal with a pregnancy all on her own. He mourned for what had happened to Lianna Dunhill all those years ago just as much as he mourned the father he never knew. "Instead of choosing, Archibald vanished. He stopped answering her calls and disappeared like a coward."

Susannah didn't speak. She didn't have to. Her silence was the softest kind of sympathy.

"That's apparently when my mom did a little digging," Oliver continued, running the pad of his thumb over the condensation that clung to his glass. "Turned out, Archibald wasn't just married to Agatha. There were two other Mrs. Fortunes—Damaris and Taffy. All three lived in different parts of the country, and they all believed they were the only one."

"Good grief," Susannah whispered, her voice hoarse with disbelief. "What kind of man—?"

"The rich, powerful kind who thought he'd never get caught." Oliver's mouth tightened. "My mom threatened to expose him. He offered her millions to stay quiet. She took it. Moved away, changed her name and started over. She was convinced she was doing the best thing for her and the baby."

Susannah's lips parted, as if to ask something, then closed again. She didn't need to say it. The question hovered between them anyway: *And until now, you never knew?*

He gave her a wry smile. "I didn't have a clue. Not until a private investigator showed up and turned my world upside down. Hired by the Fortunes, believe it or not. They'd just found out about me, thanks to Archibald's sudden death—and the triplet lawyers who read his will."

"Triplet…lawyers?" Her lips twitched, and for the first time in what felt like hours, Oliver saw a flicker of the girl he remembered.

"Yup. Because this whole situation wasn't crazy enough already," he replied with a grin. "Anyway, turns out Archibald's will had a catch. His five kids from the marriages couldn't inherit a dime until they found the one missing child he'd never acknowledged."

"So you're the key to the whole inheritance," she said slowly.

"Bingo." Oliver took a long drink of limeade before setting the jar down with a clink. "And let me tell you, that's one heck of a way to find out you have five siblings and a father who practically ran a domestic Ponzi scheme."

"It doesn't sound real. More like something out of a television melodrama. Believe me, I should know." Susannah gave a small, incredulous laugh, covering her mouth with the back of her hand. "I mean, the triplet lawyers alone…"

"Sometimes they even dress alike. It's honestly a little disturbing." Oliver pulled a face. It felt good to make her laugh, though. Just like old times.

Then her humor faded into something else—curiosity, maybe. "What's it like having five new family members?"

He hesitated, swirling the ice in his glass. "Not too bad, believe it or not. My brothers and sisters are good people. I also feel closer than ever to my mom now, if that makes sense. I wanted to know who she'd been before I came along. It wasn't easy finding anything. She changed her name and burned every bridge. But I finally traced a record back to a woman named Jeralyn Ward—her aunt. She's in a memory care facility in Bisonville."

Susannah's brows pulled together. "Is she…?"

"Alive? Yeah. Lucid? Not so much. But I visit her every Thursday anyway. I bring her flowers and sit with her by the window while she calls me Paul or Steven or her cat Pickle. None of that matters, though," he said.

Susannah's gaze turned soft as she peered at him from behind her hair. "That's kind of beautiful, Oliver."

He shrugged, a gentle smile tugging at the corner of his mouth. "She's family, and that's something I haven't had for a very long time."

If Oliver had learned the truth about his secret family years ago, he wasn't sure how he would've reacted. He was a grown man now, though—a man who'd experienced grief and loss and heartache. As painful as those things could be, they also had a way of bringing clarity and perspective that youth couldn't offer.

He dropped his gaze to the countertop, and one of the Labs—the yellow one—shuffled toward him and planted her head on Oliver's knee. He rested a hand on the dog's broad head.

"Has anyone ever told you that you've got three really great dogs?" he said, then looked up at Susannah with a smile.

"They're my best friends in the entire world." She grinned back at him, but the smile didn't quite reach her eyes.

There was no doubt in Oliver's mind that she loved

her trio of retrievers. From where he was sitting, he could see plenty of evidence, from the menagerie of dog photos stuck to the stainless steel refrigerator, to the collection of leashes hanging by the back door, to the plush pet beds scattered all over the floor. By all appearances, her life revolved around Hershey, Honey and Bear. So why was there a quiet ache hiding just behind her grin?

The realization hit him like a slow, steady weight in the center of his chest.

They're not just her best friends. They're her only *friends here in Texas.*

"Tell me more about your new family," she said, deflecting the attention away from her and back onto his drama-filled life. "Is the land next door part of your inheritance?"

"Yes, it is. I felt strange about it at first. Honestly, I wasn't even sure I wanted it, but then we found a journal buried right near the spot where Archibald wanted his ashes scattered. That's when everything changed." He gave a slight shake of his head. "For me, anyway."

Susannah's eyes narrowed slightly. *"We?"*

"My new siblings and I," he clarified. They'd wanted him to be the first to read it since he'd never had the chance to know their father. After he'd finished, he passed it along to his sisters Shelby and Jillian and they, in turn, had shared it with brothers Hayes and Penn. Madeline had been the last to read it, and now they had a big family meeting scheduled at the Emerald Ridge Hotel tomorrow to discuss the journal's contents.

"What did it say?" Susannah scrunched her face.

"Sorry, is that a nosy question? This whole story is just so fascinating."

Oliver laughed under his breath. "Not nosy at all. It actually feels good to talk about all of this with someone other than family."

Someone who wasn't tangled up in the grief and shock of it all. Someone who would just listen…and who'd known him longer than anyone else in this town.

"Archibald poured his heart out in those pages. He wrote about his past, his regrets and the things he wished he'd done differently. He knew he'd made a mess of everything, but he hoped we'd forgive him anyway. That maybe knowing how he felt at the time might make a difference."

There was more, obviously. But the heart of the story was what mattered most to Oliver.

"I guess it really did make a difference. Not right away, but…reading that journal? It made him human. And it helped me realize I didn't want to keep living as a question mark." He took a deep breath. "So I made it official."

Susannah's eyes sparkled, one corner of her mouth tugging up. "So the journal *is* the reason you took his name."

He nodded. "Oliver Fortune Dunhill, like I said. What do you think? It kind of has a ring to it, doesn't it?"

"It does. I like it." She looked him up and down, and her smile widened. "You seem…proud."

"I think I am," he returned slowly. "Not of everything that happened, but of what I'm choosing to do with it. I want to be a man who owns his story. Who doesn't hide in the shadows of his parents' mistakes. I want to believe they loved me in their own broken, tangled ways and that they were just doing the best they could."

For a long moment, the only sound was the ticking of the old wall clock and the soft hum of the glossy, retro-style refrigerator.

"Like I said earlier, you're a good son, Oliver. I'm happy for you. You deserve a new start here in Emerald Ridge," she finally said.

His heart gave a thud.

"You deserve a new start, too," he told her, his voice low, hoping he wasn't overstepping. "If that's really what you want…"

Chapter Three

"That's precisely why I'm here," Susannah said, swallowing hard. "For a fresh, new beginning."

If anyone could understand, surely Oliver could, given everything he'd just shared with her.

A new start was exactly what she wanted. As lonely as she felt at times, she knew she'd made the right decision. Out here, she had space to breathe without wondering what people were thinking when they looked at her damaged face. With all the trappings of her old life stripped away, she could focus on who she really was. She was getting to know herself again, from the inside out.

And as she did, she realized Brett had been right about something. She *had* changed.

"Can I tell you a secret?" she asked before she could stop herself.

"I just told you all about the darkest, craziest chapter of my life, Suzy Q," Oliver said, using her nickname from their summer together. Her cheeks went warm at the sound of it. "You can tell me anything."

She drew in a slow breath. "I'm writing a book."

There, she'd said it. After years of playing characters in other people's stories, she was finally working on one of her own. Until now, she hadn't told a soul. Except for Hershey, Honey and Bear, of course. Her own little tail-wagging book club.

"That's amazing." Oliver's eyes lit up like he meant it. "Let me guess… It's a mystery novel, isn't it?"

Susannah gasped. "How did you know?"

She'd been waiting for him to assume the obvious— that she was working on a tell-all autobiography. Wasn't that what all big stars did once they were past their prime?

Past your prime? You're not even thirty years old yet.

Right. Well, age had nothing to do with it. Like it or not, she was stuck in some horrid, alternate version of her favorite fairy tale, *Beauty and the Beast*. And— spoiler alert!—she'd been cast as the Beast.

Oliver grinned at her, seemingly still under the impression she was the Beauty. "If memory serves, you read the entire Nancy Drew series that summer."

"That's right!" She felt herself smile. The resort where their families had stayed near Barton Creek had a library stuffed with old books. The signature yellow spines of the hardback Nancy Drew series had stretched across two full shelves. "I can't believe you remember that."

"How could I forget? I was going to be the Ned Nickerson to your Nancy Drew," he said with a wink. "Except you never needed rescuing."

How times change…

Her throat grew thick, and once again, she wished

she could turn back the clock. Except instead of returning to her old life in Hollywood, she'd go all the way back to summer at the lake. Sunburned and barefoot, with the whole world ahead of them.

"I bet your book is incredible. I'd love to read it sometime," Oliver said.

"It's not finished quite yet. Soon, though." She swallowed. "Hopefully."

He winked. "It's a date, then."

Her breath hitched at his casual use of the word *date*. It probably meant nothing—just a figure of speech—but it still sent a flutter through her chest that she wasn't prepared for. Vulnerability edged in, sharp and unwelcome. She wasn't ready for flutters. *Not yet.*

She gave a small, uncertain cough. "Are you related to Madeline Fortune?"

He frowned for a beat at the sudden change of subject, but kept his tone light. "She's one of my new half-siblings, actually. Why?"

"She's been trying to get in touch with me for months—calling and leaving notes. She even showed up at my gate a while back. I still haven't responded. I thought if I ignored her long enough, she'd give up, but I'm beginning to wonder." Susannah's bottom lip slipped between her teeth. The thing with Madeline Fortune had become a real problem. She hated to be rude, but couldn't the woman take a hint?

"Madeline is persistent," Oliver said with a chuckle. "Do you know why she's trying to get in touch?"

"She's after me to attend a party she's planning for Kate Fortune's hundredth birthday. I haven't seen Kate in years. She's my great-great-aunt through marriage, but there was a big falling-out. It all happened fifteen years ago, some awful family mess between my mother, my grandmother and Kate. I was only thirteen and stuck right in the middle of it."

"I'm a Fortune now, remember?" He let out a quiet laugh. "I know all about the party, and that Madeline is desperately trying to get Kate's long-lost niece to attend, but she's a recluse."

Recluse? Was that what people were calling her now?

If the shoe fits, she thought with a pang.

She raised her hand. "Hi, I'm the recluse, it's me."

Oliver's expression softened. She'd been trying to sound funny and self-deprecating, but he'd seen right through the act. "I'm sorry. I shouldn't have used that word. You caught me by surprise, that's all."

"It's fine. I guess there are only so many no-trespassing and private-property signs you can put up before people start using that word." Not to mention the disguises she used every time she ventured off her ranch, but perhaps those were better left unacknowledged. For now, anyway.

"When was the last time you saw your Aunt Kate?" Oliver asked.

"I don't even remember. How sad is that?" Susannah shook her head and sighed. "My mom and grandma died in a car accident two years after the big falling-out, and my dad forbade me from ever seeing Kate again. He said it's what Mom would've wanted, and I've respected that. I was just a kid, you know? Even after he passed, I just never reached out. Now it just feels like it's too late."

Oliver was silent for a beat, allowing the story to settle between them. Then he dipped his head to catch her gaze. "It's never too late, Suzy. Look at you and me, reconnecting after all this time."

"That's different." *You're different. You're safe. You always have been...* "I've been ignoring Madeline's requests because I'm not ready to be part of society again. I might *never* be ready. All I really want is to be left alone."

She drew in a long breath and glanced out the window at the sunlight filtering through the tree branches. "I have good memories of Kate, I do. But I doubt she's given me more than a passing thought in all these years."

"That's not true," Oliver said gently. "Quite the opposite, actually. According to Madeline, all Kate wants for her birthday is for you to be there. Reconnecting with you means everything to her. And she's turning one hundred, Suzy. She might not have many more birthdays left."

Susannah's heart winced with guilt. She just wasn't sure she could do it. "There'll be so many people there. Hundreds, probably. I can't just walk into a room like that. Not the way I am now."

Oliver nodded but didn't say anything, and his silence spoke volumes. He was right, and Susannah knew it.

"Maybe I'll reconsider." She took a deep breath. "But if I do go, I'll have to wear a disguise. Large sunglasses and a wide-rimmed hat, maybe. Something to hide my face."

His voice was calm and steady, such a sharp contrast to the storm swirling in the pit of her stomach. "I understand. But if you decide to go, I promise to be right there beside you the entire time if it helps."

Again, Susannah felt a flicker of something she hadn't dared name in so long—safety. "No matter what your name is, you're still the same kind boy who gave me my first kiss. Aren't you, Oliver Fortune Dunhill?"

The words were out before she could stop them. Her eyes widened, and she quickly turned her face, letting her hair fall like a curtain over her scar.

"Suzy Q?" he murmured so softly that she barely heard it over the pounding of her heart.

She hesitated before looking at him, just barely.

"Make no mistake—you're still the beautiful girl I first met all those summers ago." He reached for her face but stopped short of touching her, fingertips tracing the air just a whisper away from her cheek. Somehow it felt every bit as real as a caress. "Your scar and the other physical reminders of your accident are part of you now, but you're *still* you. Trust me, everything about you is still lovely, inside and out, just like when we were lovesick kids."

Lovesick kids.

Susannah couldn't help but smile. The memories of those days were sugar-kissed and infused with warm, golden sunshine. She wished going back there was as simple as whipping up a batch of limeade.

The way Oliver talked almost made it seem possible.

When he told her she was lovely, it sounded real—not like a lie. If she squeezed her eyes closed tight enough, she just might believe him.

"I wish I could stay and talk longer," he said, and just like that, the magic spell was broken. "I'd sit here with you until the sun went down if I could. But I've got a meeting soon. There's a cattle ranch nearby I'm thinking of buying. Now that I've got this whole new family—five siblings and three stepmothers—I want to put some roots down in Emerald Ridge."

She didn't want him to go. Maybe it was misguided or foolish to trust him since they hadn't seen each other in so long, but she *did* trust him. After the year she'd had, it felt like a miracle, and she wasn't ready for it to end. Not yet…

"Would you like to come over for dinner tomorrow night?" she asked before she could second-guess herself.

And then it happened. Oliver looked up, surprised, and when he smiled at her, it was the exact same smile he'd given her the day he offered to share his Popsicle. All at once, the world went sticky sweet and Susannah's biggest worry wasn't her face or her limp or the deeper, invisible scars that cut her to the quick. It was whether or not Oliver might kiss her during the Fourth of July fireworks over the cool waters of Barton Creek and whether her knees might actually give out if he did.

"I'd like that a lot," he said.

She blinked and couldn't quite tell where the past left off and the present began. It all swirled together like a dreamy watercolor painting.

"It's a date, then." She echoed his words from earlier—except then, they'd been talking in hypotheticals. This time, it was real.

She had a date with Oliver Fortune Dunhill, and they were all grown up now. Over a decade after they'd last seen each other, it was finally happening…

Ready or not.

Chapter Four

Sun poured through the wide windows of the Emerald Ridge Hotel's meeting room the following morning, casting golden light across the polished hardwood floors. Ceiling fans turned lazily overhead, stirring the warm air scented faintly with lemon oil and roses from the garden just beyond the patio doors. The Fortune siblings and their mothers had gathered in a loose circle around the conference table where Archibald's journal sat like an open wound.

Oliver stood near the French doors, looking out over the hotel's sprawling lawn. Beyond it, wildflowers bloomed along the fence line, and bees hovered lazily in the still air. Everything looked so peaceful and serene. But inside the room, emotions simmered like one of Texas's legendary thunderstorms rolling across the expansive sky, thick and ready to break.

"We've read it now," Oliver said, turning back to face his siblings and their mothers. He was the only one standing—the oddball, as usual. As much as he wanted a relationship with these people, he still wasn't sure where or how he fit in. "What did you all think?"

The room was quiet for a beat too long.

The others were situated around the table, grouped by family. Agatha Fortune, Archibald's original wife, twisted a handkerchief as she sat between her daughters, Shelby and Jillian. Across from them, wife number two from Houston, Damaris Fortune, was flanked by her sons, Hayes and Penn. Archibald's third wife, Taffy, sighed beside her daughter, Madeline. Taffy and Madeline had been living in a flashy Dallas suburb when Archibald passed away, which tracked. The only thing bigger than Taffy's platinum hair were her overly dramatic eyelash extensions. Oliver could feel the breeze off them every time she blinked.

Agatha was the first to speak, a trembling softness in her voice. "This is all such a surprise. Archibald never talked about his childhood, and he could be so stoic at times. It was obvious he had control issues, so I knew something wasn't quite right about the way he'd grown up. But this—"

Her eyes filled with tears as she waved her handkerchief toward the journal.

Jillian patted her mother's shoulder. "I know, Mom. I think we're all in shock."

Oliver certainly was. He'd never suspected that someone like Archibald Fortune, the workaholic CEO and founder of Fortune Air, had been born into devastating poverty on the exact tract of land he'd left to Oliver.

Oliver couldn't stop thinking about how much that acreage had meant to his father—what it had symbolized and why he'd worked so hard to buy it back after his dad had gambled it away. The journal was filled with memories written in Archibald's shaky hand, and the story began right there on the parcel of land by the railroad tracks. His parents had been dirt-poor ranchers. Archibald's father had gambling debts that ultimately led to the loss of all his assets, including his family name. When the ranch was foreclosed on, Archibald and his parents had nowhere else to go, so they moved into the woods. As hard as it was to believe, Archibald Fortune had grown up without a roof over his head.

Hayes leaned back in his leather chair, dark eyes fixed on the ceiling fan. "Living in barns. Stealing food. Sleeping in hunting cabins with wild animals during winter…and no one knew."

"Not even us," Madeline said with a wobble in her voice.

"No one," Penn agreed. "He carried it all alone."

"I keep thinking about the time he came to career day at my school," Shelby said slowly. "At first he said no, but I begged and begged, and he finally agreed. I expected him to stand quietly at the back of the room, like he usually did at public events. But he didn't. He gave my class a whole speech about perseverance, about the Fortune legacy." A soft, nostalgic look crossed her face. "He took me out for ice cream afterward, and I remember feeling so proud to be his daughter. That day has always been one of my favorite childhood memories. All this time, I thought he was talking about *his* legacy. About building businesses. But all along he meant the kind of perseverance where you steal eggs from nests just to survive the week."

Damaris's lips curved into a sad smile. "Maybe he meant both. That man built everything himself—from *nothing*. And he never told anyone. Not even his wives."

"He should have," Penn said, his voice tight with grief and something that almost sounded like admiration. "He should have told us."

Oliver shifted from one booted foot to the other. His emotions had been all over the place since learning his father's identity. He knew his siblings were grieving—not just for their dad, but for the lives they'd had before finding out that their father was a trigamist. It was like the world slipped off its axis when Archibald had his heart attack. Oliver felt for them. He really did.

But on some level, he also envied them. Just the tiniest bit.

At least you knew him.

That was the thought that kept barreling its way to the forefront of Oliver's mind every time he got together with the family. He'd had to bite his tongue to keep from saying it out loud the day they'd spread Archibald's ashes at the river. They'd known what he was thinking, though. That's why they'd insisted he should be the first to read the journal.

Now, Oliver finally knew the truth. He had no reason to envy his brothers and sisters, because they *hadn't* known their dad. Not really. No one had. Which was worse? Growing up without a father, or being raised by a man who kept the people he loved at arm's length and never let them see who he really was?

"Three families," Shelby murmured. "Three homes. Constant travel. He made it so none of us ever knew about each other because that's what safety looked like to him. Never being truly vulnerable, not even with the people he loved."

The journal sat in the center of the table, its cracked leather cover and pages filled with slanted handwriting now etched into all their memories. Inside, it chronicled a life so far removed from the luxury the Fortunes had grown up with that it felt fictional at times.

Until Oliver had read the details. Bruised knuckles from fighting off bigger boys at the rail yards. The tiny makeshift shelter his father had built with nothing more than rotted logs and stolen tarps. His mother's cough that grew worse through a brutal winter, the pages stained with ink blurred by what could only be tears.

Mere months after Archibald's mother passed away from what sounded like untreated pneumonia, his father died in a drunken accident. At fourteen, he'd become an orphan. He continued doing whatever he needed to do to survive, fending for himself to try and avoid ending up in foster care. Archibald described going without food for days at a time until he found work as a ranch hand at a place that turned a blind eye to his age. What followed was the most remarkable part of the story, at least to Oliver.

Archibald worked his fingers to the bone on that ranch. He scrimped and saved, and the first thing he did once he'd built a little nest egg was buy back the family land that his father had lost—the land that now belonged to Oliver.

His throat closed up tight every time he thought about that part of the journal. He'd read the story so many times that he knew the words by heart, and the passages spun round and round in his head every time he took a step on that land. That's why he'd been doing so much walking lately. The property was sacred ground. All the answers he'd been searching for were right there—in the soil his grandfather had tilled, in the wind that whispered through the cedar trees, in the quiet echoes of a life he never got to witness but somehow felt all around him.

Oliver would never know his father face-to-face. He'd never hear his laugh or feel what it was like for his dad to ruffle his hair when he hit a home run in Little League. But now, he knew Archibald's heart, and even though he had never followed through on his promise to marry his mother, he knew his father had never forgotten him. In his own way, Archibald had loved him all along. The land proved it.

"I've been angry at him for such a long time," Taffy said, and for once, her words were laced with tenderness instead of hatred. Oliver hadn't known her long, obviously, but she'd made her feelings about her late husband's polygamy clear. Not only that, for a while she'd even tried to dig up dirt on all the other wives so she could increase her share of the inheritance. As if there wasn't enough of Archibald's millions to go around. "Not just since the heart attack and the humiliation of learning that all of you existed."

Across from her, Hayes cleared his throat.

"No offense," Taffy added with a flick of her glossy manicure.

Agatha sat up a little straighter and muttered under her breath, "None taken."

"I knew he was up to something. I suspected affairs—lots of them. It never occurred to me that he might have multiple families." Taffy sighed. "But the way he writes about all of us almost makes it sound…"

She let her voice drift off.

"Normal?" Oliver offered with an arch of a single eyebrow.

Taffy glared at him, but it lacked its usual sting. "Nothing about this entire situation will *ever* be normal."

"The reason Dad had three families—" Shelby cast Oliver a meaningful glance "—along with you and your mother too, obviously—was because he knew it meant he'd never be alone. He said so himself." She stared at the journal for a beat and then swallowed. "He lost so much at such a young age. He never wanted to feel alone again."

"His reasons were heartbreaking. That doesn't mean his choices didn't hurt, but it makes them a little bit easier to understand. That's what you were trying to say, wasn't it, Mom?" Madeline cast a watery smile at Taffy. "It's okay to feel sad and angry at the same time."

"I'm not sure I want to be angry anymore," her mother said quietly, and the room fell silent again.

Outside, the drone of a lawn mower started in the distance. A bright red cardinal landed briefly on the windowsill before fluttering away.

"I forgive him," Jillian said softly. "Not because what he did was okay. But because I can't read those pages and not see the boy he was. The boy who grew into a man doing the best he knew how."

Shelby nodded. "Me, too."

Oliver, Agatha and Madeline agreed, followed by Hayes and Penn. Then there was another long pause before Taffy finally said, "Fine—I forgive him. I don't know what I'll do with all the rage, but I'll try not to let it define him anymore."

Damaris's voice broke slightly. "I'm getting there…"

Oliver looked around at his siblings and their mothers, each of them carrying pieces of a man they had only just begun to understand. A father who had loved deeply, but imperfectly. Who had wanted to protect them all, by keeping them apart.

"He wasn't just the man who made mistakes," Oliver said quietly. "He was the kid who walked barefoot down dirt roads, looking for scraps. He was the teen who lied about his age just to earn enough to eat. He was the man who wanted so badly to belong that he fractured himself to do it."

"We're the pieces he left behind," Penn concurred. "All of us."

Hayes took a deep breath. "There's still so much we don't know. I'm sure there will always be things we don't understand about our dad, but for now, this is enough. It is for me, anyway."

Oliver nodded. And then, one by one, the Fortune children and their mothers said their goodbyes, not just to the man who had left them with secrets and scars, but to the version of him they thought they knew.

The powerful, polished tycoon. The smooth-talking father. The elusive husband.

Now, in his place, stood a boy in the woods, a young man covered in dust and sweat, a dreamer with blistered hands who built something no one thought possible.

How had that boy come to start the country's most profitable airline? It seemed impossible…

Almost as implausible as the fact that Oliver's mother had been lying to him for his entire life. The journal had answered a lot of his questions, but not *all* of them, and now that both his parents were gone, those answers seemed more elusive than ever.

Oliver turned the journal over in his hands and ran the pad of his thumb over the worn leather cover. No one had picked it up on their way out, so he tucked it under his arm and took it with him. If none of his siblings wanted to volunteer to be the keeper of their father's secrets, he was willing. In a way, it seemed fitting. Oliver's entire life had been wrapped up in secrets, since the day he was born.

An empty feeling nagged at him as he made his way out of the meeting room and walked through the hotel lobby. He'd hoped this morning's gathering would bring him a sense of closure, and, in a way, it had with regard to Archibald. But like Taffy said, nothing about this situation would ever be normal. Oliver had come to Emerald Ridge to learn more about his past and where he'd come from, but nothing could've prepared him for what he'd learned. Not just about his dad, but about his mother, too.

He and Mom had always had such a close relationship, but the more he found out about her past, the more he realized that he never really knew her at all. She lied about their identities because she was scared. The only reason Archibald had given her millions of dollars was because she'd discovered his dirty little secret and threatened to expose him to all three of his wives. She probably thought he might send someone after her to get the money back. Or worse.

Oliver blinked hard. He didn't like to think about his mom on the run alone and pregnant. At the same time, he didn't understand why she'd never told him the truth. He wouldn't have judged her. She had to know that. He *loved* his mother, but in the end, her whole life had been a lie.

Just like Archibald's.

Oliver hadn't been lying when he'd told Susannah that he felt closer to Lianna Dunhill now that he knew the truth. Still, his faith in people had taken a bit of a hit.

Back when Oliver first started doing ranch work, he met a trainer who regularly used blinders on horses while doing harness work or around potential hazards. Limiting a horse's peripheral vision helped reduce distractions and make them less responsive to stressful stimuli in their environment. It helped the horse feel more secure. Oliver wasn't a fan of limiting a horse's natural vision, and he never used blinders on his own ranch. One of the reasons was because he'd seen what happened when the trainer took the blinders off. The horse inevitably became disoriented at the sudden change. Some horses even panicked.

Now that the dust had settled on his family drama, Oliver felt the same way. The blinders were off, and he wasn't sure how to react to this new, broader field of vision. Was *everyone* lying about who they were? Was there anyone at all he could trust?

"Oliver, hey!" someone called, jerking him out of his thoughts and back to the here and now.

He stumbled to a halt directly in front of Madeline, who'd apparently been darting back into the hotel just as he'd been about to walk out.

"Hi, Mads. Sorry I almost bumped into you." He clutched the journal tighter under his arm. "I guess I've got a lot on my mind."

"We all do. No need to apologize." She blew out a breath and then pointed to the leather book. "Oh, good—you got it. I realized no one had picked up Dad's journal, and I came back to make sure we hadn't accidentally left it behind."

"Did you want to take it?" He offered it to her.

She shook her head, and her long red hair shone like a shiny copper penny. "You keep it. I think you should have it. Maybe if you build a cabin or something on the land, you can tuck it on a bookshelf there. That seems fitting, don't you think?"

"To keep the journal where we found it, so to speak?" Oliver gave a slow nod. "You're right. That was a special place to Archibald. It belongs there."

She smoothed down the front of her silk skirt. "I

was hoping you'd agree. Have you made any plans for the land yet, now that you've decided to stay here in Emerald Ridge?"

"I'm still deciding. I looked at a ranch for sale around here yesterday, but now I'm dragging my feet making a decision. Part of me wants to develop Archibald's land instead. But that would take a lot of work."

The ranch for sale that he'd toured last night would be ideal, but making an offer just hadn't felt right. It might take him a year or more to get a working cattle operation fully up and running on the acreage he'd inherited, but he couldn't stop thinking about honoring the grandparents he'd never known by turning the land where they'd had such humble beginnings into someplace special. Maybe he had more in common with Archibald than he realized. His father had been a dreamer. Reclaiming the family land had been part of the big plans he made for his future, and now Oliver was tempted to follow in those same footsteps.

"I think that's a great idea. Really, I do." Madeline's expression softened, full of sisterly fondness. "Listen, I don't know if any of the others have said this to you yet, but Dad would've been proud of you, Oliver. The fact that you want to stay and build a life here would've made him really happy. Doubly so, if you did it on the land where he grew up."

"Thank you. I'm actually really glad we're getting a chance to talk for a minute, just the two of us." He adjusted the rim of his Stetson and lowered his voice. The Emerald Ridge Hotel was a popular spot for tourists looking to relax in luxe accommodations in the resort town. He didn't want anyone to overhear. "The funniest thing happened yesterday. I ran into Susannah Simmons."

Madeline's mouth dropped open. "You *ran into her*? How on earth did that happen? I've been trying to contact her for weeks without any luck at all."

"We know each other, believe it or not," he said.

His sister's stunned expression cranked up a notch or two. "You know Susannah Simmons? She's *mega* famous. Why haven't you mentioned it?"

Oliver's gut churned. He wasn't sure how he felt about the fame part—not when he had a date with her later tonight. Yesterday, she'd seemed like the same girl he'd known so long ago. *His Suzy Q.*

But he was a realist now. That tended to happen to a person after they'd been slapped hard in the face by reality the way Oliver recently had. Trust didn't come so easily these days. He'd learned the hard way that people weren't always who they said they were.

He swallowed. "I've been a little busy sorting out my entire life history lately. That seems like something you might understand."

Madeline winced. "Sorry—I get it. I've been here in Emerald Ridge longer than you have, too. It's just that she's *Susannah Simmons*. How on earth do you two know each other?"

She was my first kiss.

Oliver didn't dare say it. But since yesterday, he couldn't get that kiss out of his head. They'd been kids, obviously, and hadn't really known what they were doing. But the aching tenderness he'd felt when her lips grazed his had never gone away. He'd been so young then, so innocent. He wasn't sure he'd ever kissed anyone with his heart so open wide, other than Suzy. The vulnerability was what made it beautiful, and it was also what haunted him. Oliver was all grown up now, hardened not just by years, but by the heartbreak and name changes and quiet disappointments that had slowly chipped away at the openness he once carried like second nature.

He rubbed the back of his neck, suddenly aware of how close the past felt. "We met one summer when we were fourteen, both in Austin on vacation with our families. It was a long time ago."

Madeline's lips quirked into a curious grin. "That's wild, Oliver."

"Anyway… I was out walking my property line yesterday, trying to process everything, and I must have wandered too far. Her dogs tracked me down and made a commotion. It turns out Susannah's remote ranch borders my land."

Madeline's eyes widened as she looked him up and down. "Did the dogs hurt you? They sounded pretty ferocious when Hayes and I were there."

Those softies of Susannah's? He couldn't help but laugh. "Hardly. They're Labs, and all three of them are as sweet as pie."

His sister tilted her head, eyes narrowing. "That's so odd. Her ranch is basically a fortress. I was imagining police dogs or something."

"Yeah, no. I'm willing to bet the barking you heard was part of her alarm system. Her security is top-notch.

There's no way her pack could scare you like that." He shook his head, still chuckling. "Susannah invited me in and we got caught up on our lives. It was nice. When she heard I was a Fortune now, she mentioned Kate's party. I think I might have convinced her to attend. She's not one hundred percent, but she's considering it. Maybe don't mention it to Kate yet, just in case."

"Oliver!" Madeline threw her arms around him. "This is *amazing*. Thank you so much. If you pull this off, you'll be a lifesaver."

"I'll see what I can do," he said, meeting her hopeful gaze as she pulled back to grin at him. A playful spark danced in her eyes, and he got the feeling her excitement had to do with more than just Kate Fortune's one-hundredth birthday party. "What's that look for, Mads?"

"Your entire face lit up the second you mentioned Susannah." She jabbed a pointer finger at his chest and winked. "That doesn't happen often. You're a bit of a closed book, Oliver Fortune Dunhill."

If that was true, at least he'd come by it honestly.

"You and Susannah Simmons. I still can't believe it. Could romance be in the air?" Madeline asked, waggling her brows with exaggerated flair.

Oliver removed his hat, dragged a hand through his hair and then jammed the Stetson back on his head.

"Don't start," he said, chuckling despite himself.

But if Oliver had learned anything in recent months, it was that anything was possible.

Chapter Five

A few hours later, Oliver stood on the front porch of Susannah's luxurious log mansion, clutching a bouquet of daisies. When he'd bought the flowers at Emerald Ridge Floral on the way home from his family meeting earlier, he'd told himself it was just a polite gesture since Suzy had invited him back to her home. He wasn't a trespasser this go-round—he was an invited guest.

But the fact that he'd insisted on daisies was a dead giveaway. He knew good and well what those flowers meant. Humble, handpicked daisies had been all he'd had to offer Susannah when they were kids. The bouquet was steeped in the best kind of nostalgia. But now that he was here on her doorstep, he wondered if she'd even remember. Would it look like he'd stopped at the corner store and picked up the cheapest thing he could get his hands on? Susannah was "mega famous" now, as Madeline had so unceremoniously said this morning when she'd found out they knew each other. She'd probably received hundreds, if not thousands, of elaborate bouquets in the years since he'd picked her daisies. He was pretty sure he'd seen pictures of her at some film premiere, clutching an enormous bouquet of velvety roses on the red carpet while her handsome costar beamed beside her. The guy had also been one of those faces that Madeline would recognize without needing a name. All perfect hair and smug confidence, the kind of man who probably had a publicist and a personal trainer instead of a messy family history and a pile of secrets he didn't know what to do with.

Maybe Oliver should've gone with a more upscale flower selection like the clerk at the florist had not so subtly suggested. Emerald Ridge Floral was high-end enough that she'd had to go to the back room to search for the modest flowers he'd inquired about. But then, she'd returned with a bundle of daisies tied with a blue gingham bow and asked him if he knew that the sweet white flowers were supposed to symbolize purity, innocence and new beginnings. Oliver was sold, right there on the spot.

A soft snort echoed from the narrow gap between the heavy wooden door and its frame. *Busted.* The dogs obviously knew he was there. The time to rethink his floral decisions was long gone.

Suddenly, the door swung open, and Susannah stood on the threshold with her hair in a loose braid over one shoulder and a smile tugging at her lips.

"Hey, cowboy." She stepped aside to let him in.

"Evening, ma'am," he said in an exaggerated drawl as the three Labradors gathered around him to sniff his boots.

Susannah laughed. "Sorry. They must smell your animals. Do you have a dog?"

"No, but I've got several hundred head of cattle and half a dozen horses back on my ranch in Austin." Oliver lifted an eyebrow. "Do they count?"

She aimed an amused glance at the Labs, who were still performing a thorough investigation of Oliver's entire person. "The pups seem to think so."

Honey was the first to lift her head. She wagged her tail and her mouth curved into a wide doggy grin. Oliver bent down to rub her behind the ears and all at once, the others jostled forward, angling for pats.

"I think they remember me," he said with a chuckle.

"I'm sure they do," Susannah replied, a hint of pink touching her cheeks. "You're kind of unforgettable."

And just like that, Oliver forgot all about the film premieres and handsome costars. It was just the two of them again. Oren and Suzy. Memories swirled between them, dappled and golden as sunlight through pine trees.

Then Bear poked his muzzle into the daisy blossoms and tried to sneak a nibble.

Oliver laughed under his breath as he stood and offered Susannah the bouquet. "I should probably give these to you before someone eats them."

"Thank you." A shy smile flickered across her features. "Daisies are my favorite."

Satisfaction settled over him. It was good to know that some things never changed, even amid life's challenges that neither of them could've predicted.

"Come join me in the kitchen. I'm still getting dinner ready." She waved for him to follow her as she padded barefoot over the soft throw rugs that covered the knotty pine floor. Bubblegum-pink toenails peeked out from the hem of her faded jeans. "I hope you're hungry."

The air was rich with something savory. Garlic, herbs…rosemary, maybe. Whatever it was smelled incredible. Hershey, Honey and Bear trotted alongside them as they passed an expansive living room with high timbered ceilings and windows overlooking the dense, green forest. The space felt so homey that it was easy to forget the log home was technically a mansion.

"Can I do anything to help?" Oliver offered as they arrived back in the kitchen where they'd shared limeade the day before.

Susannah filled a hobnail glass vase with water at the sink and began arranging the daisies. Oliver liked how she'd filled her home with timeless pieces instead of new, trendy decor. The hobnail vase, the weathered rocking chair on the porch, even the lace curtains that caught the breeze—each item told a story. They made the house feel lived-in, cherished.

"How good are you at chopping vegetables?" she asked.

He eyed the knife and cutting board situated atop the island, piled with red and orange bell peppers. "Passable. I can't promise the slices won't be uneven."

"Perfect." She grinned. "I like a little chaos."

He picked up the knife and watched her hands move gently, *expertly*, as she tucked a wayward stem back into place. "This place suits you, you know."

Something warm flickered in her expression. "You think?"

"Absolutely." He nodded and sliced into one of the peppers. "Do you ever miss your life in Hollywood?"

Yesterday, she'd told him she'd come to Texas for a fresh start, and she'd made it clear she wasn't ready to go out in public. But her quiet ranch in Emerald Ridge was a world away from the glitz and glamour of show business. The slower pace had to be a major adjustment.

"Honestly?" She shrugged, her loose braid slipping over her shoulder and falling in a soft line down the center of her back. "Not really. Fame comes at a cost, and it's one I'm no longer willing to pay."

Oliver paused for a beat and then asked quietly, "And you didn't leave anyone special behind back in California?"

He needed to know before he got any more emotionally invested than he already was. Although, whom was he kidding? His life was currently more tangled up than a barbed wire fence in a windstorm. He didn't have any business dragging someone else into his messy circus of a family—especially someone who was feeling as vulnerable as Susannah. She'd said she liked a little chaos, but he was pretty sure that was just a joke. The scar on her face caught the light when she turned her head, a physical reminder that life had already taken a swing at her once. The last thing he wanted was to add to her pain.

Susannah's smile froze as she stirred an enameled Dutch oven full of marinara sauce on the stove. She didn't say anything until the sauce began to bubble furiously.

"No one special," she mumbled as she turned down the gas. Her gaze remained glued to her wooden spoon. "I mean, there was…until the accident."

Oliver felt himself frown. Surely she didn't mean that the way it sounded.

"I was involved with my talent manager for a while. We were engaged, actually." She swallowed so hard he could hear the click of it over the bubbling sauce. Her knuckles whitened around the spoon.

"He said he loved me. Told me I was his whole world. But after the accident…" She finally looked up, her eyes glossy with the sheen of memories she'd rather forget. "He saw the scars and disappeared. Just like that."

Oliver's heart twisted. His hands curled into fists at his sides, a flash of anger sparking low in his chest. The thought of anyone walking away from her because of something so shallow made his blood burn. "Susannah—"

She shook her head, a small, sad smile curving her lips. "It's fine. I don't blame him anymore. He told me he felt like I'd become a whole different person than I was before the wreck, and truthfully, he was right."

The sauce simmered quietly now, filling the kitchen with the scent of garlic and tomatoes. But the warmth in the air couldn't thaw the chill settling in Oliver's chest. "Still, that had to hurt. I'm sorry."

"What about you?" she asked as she placed the wooden spoon on a spoon rest and wiped her hands on a dish towel. Oliver couldn't blame her for wanting to swiftly move on from the topic of her ex, even though he felt like there was probably a lot more to unpack about the breakup. "Is there anyone special in your life?"

"No," he said with a wry smile. "Just me and those hundreds of cows I mentioned earlier."

She laughed, though a shadow of wistfulness clung to her expression. Oliver got the distinct feeling that whatever her former fiancé had said to her after the accident had cut deeper than any scar. "And you're really thinking about moving the entire operation here to Emerald Ridge? That sounds like a gigantic undertaking."

"It's a process, that's for sure." First off, he'd have to sell his ranch in Austin, and that was likely to take six months, minimum. At least that would give him enough time to get the new land operational.

"Does this mean your meeting last night was a success? Are you going to make an offer on the spread you looked at?"

Oliver set the knife down on the cutting board. The bell peppers lay in neat strips, their bright colors vivid against the grain of the wood. "I'm not sure, actually. The property was nice. It reminds me a lot of my ranch in Austin, but I'm starting to think that might not be a good thing."

He glanced at her, then out the kitchen window toward the tree-covered hills. "Being here in Emerald Ridge makes me want to do things differently. My current business is very corporate. That means big profits, obviously, but it also means a lot of time behind a desk, along with too many business trips and too much time away. I've let other folks handle most of the day-to-day stuff for a long time now."

If the ranch hadn't been able to run itself, Oliver wouldn't have had the time to come down here and dig around in his mother's past. He might never have learned that he was a Fortune or where he'd come from. He felt settled now, though—physically, any-way. Wasn't there an old saying about where your body is, your heart will follow? If not, there should be.

"I want to change up my business model so it's smaller scale, more hands-on. I want to work the land myself, raise the cattle with my own two hands and build something real. Something lasting. I'm think-ing the best place to do that might be on the family land I inherited."

When he swiveled his attention back to Susannah, the light had returned to her eyes. It wasn't the guarded expression he'd come to expect from her, but something softer…fuller, more vibrant. "So right next door, then?"

"Right next door," he confirmed, his gaze steady on hers.

"You always did want to be a cowboy, just like I al-ways wanted to be a mystery author." Something tender stirred in her expression. "Look at us. It took a while, but we're both chasing after the desires of our hearts."

"How did you get into acting, anyway?" he asked.

"My mother." She gave a small, wistful laugh. "She pushed me into it, actually. Commercial auditions, beauty pageants, local talent shows—you name it. By the time I was a teenager, she had me driving all over the city for casting calls."

Her gaze drifted away for a moment. "Aunt Kate hated it. She thought Mom was pushing me too hard, treating it like her dream instead of mine. That's what started their big rift."

A gentle quiet settled between them, not awkward but comfortable. Ripe with unspoken things. He found himself holding on to every word, grateful she trusted him enough to share pieces of herself he hadn't heard before.

The thing she'd said about them both chasing after the desires of their hearts had burrowed under his skin, and he couldn't let it go. What Oliver's heart desired most of all right then was *her*. He knew she wasn't ready to hear that yet, though. He wasn't even sure he was ready to say it. They didn't really know each other anymore.

But on a soul-deep level, he knew that wasn't true. Susannah just might know him better than anyone. The realization hit with unexpected force—how easily she could still read him. It was both unsettling and achingly right. There was a comfort in it and a pull that almost felt like coming home.

So he took a step closer to her, and then another, moving with care in case she wasn't ready. He heard her breath hitch, but it was the sound of anticipation, not fear or hesitancy. And when he placed his hands against the counter on either side of her, caging her in, the air between them hummed with a tender tension. Susannah lifted her chin to look him square in the eyes. No more hiding behind her beautiful hair, no more walls. Oliver could feel the warmth radiating from her, and he recognized that quiet intake of breath for what it really was—an invitation.

"Kiss me, cowboy," she whispered.

He dipped his head, and just before their lips met, he murmured, "I thought you'd never ask."

And the moment his mouth came down on hers, time unraveled. The years between the last time he'd kissed her and now slipped away. All at once, it was the same, but different. Softer. Sweeter. *Better.* She didn't taste like cherry lip gloss and limeade anymore, but holding her was still like capturing golden sunlight in his hands…like running barefoot through tall grass. Oliver had waited a lifetime of summers to kiss her again, and the wait had been worth every excruciating second.

Then came the jingle of a collar and dog tags, followed by a happy woof. Hershey poked his broad head between them, and then the other two Labs followed suit, as if trying to wedge their way into a group hug.

Susannah laughed against Oliver's lips. He pulled back a fraction to arch an eyebrow at the canine trio. "And here I thought you guys were too friendly to be bodyguards."

"You'd better watch out. Hurt me, and they'll eat you alive," Susannah warned with mock solemnity.

"I would never hurt you, Suzy Q," he said with a wink. "That's a promise sealed with a kiss, no matter what these monsters think."

Then he gave her a light peck on the cheek, right near the corner of her scar. Her fingertips fluttered to her face like she'd forgotten all about the painful reminder of the worst day of her life.

With a lump in his throat, Oliver realized that for a brief, blissful moment, he'd made her feel safe again. Maybe even adored. No matter what happened from here on out, that small triumph was something that no one else could take away—not Susannah's boisterous canine crew, not the prying eyes of the public that terrified her so much, not even her idiot ex.

Still, a shadow lingered beneath the warmth. His own life was a mess, built on lies he felt like he was only beginning to untangle. After learning that his mother had hidden the truth and that his father had lived multiple secret lives, trust didn't come naturally anymore. The ground beneath him still felt unsteady, shifting with every new revelation.

And yet, somehow, being here with her made him want to find solid footing again.

They ate dinner on the back porch of the big log house at the farmhouse table where Susannah liked to sit in the mornings and work on her mystery novel. Summers in Texas were always sweltering, but the dense trees surrounding her ranch helped, and it was still early enough in the season to catch a cool breeze during the morning twilight and the evening hours.

"It's beautiful out here, Suzy," Oliver said as he uncorked the bottle of crisp white wine that she'd kept chilling in a vintage hammered copper ice bucket.

"Yeah, I spend as much time on the porch as I can." She took the glass he handed her and gave her wine a gentle swirl. "It was one of my favorite things about this house the first time I saw it."

The porch stretched wide across the rear of the log mansion, made from thick timber beams that still carried the scent of pine when the sun warmed them. Heavy wooden columns supported the overhanging roof, where huge hanging ferns swayed gently in the damp air. Planters filled with herbs and trailing wild-flowers lined the steps, and a hand-built stone path curved toward the area where Susannah planned to build a small garden. Since she'd gotten into cooking, she snipped herbs nearly every day. She liked the idea of maybe adding vegetables to the mix, too. When she really let herself get carried away with her daydreaming, she pictured a small chicken coop tucked along the path—the kind with a slanted tin roof and a hand-painted sign. She imagined collecting fresh eggs in the mornings before walking the dogs and the soft cluck of hens as calming background noise for her writing sessions.

But surely, Oliver wasn't interested in hearing about all that, even if he was looking at her like every dream she'd ever had was worth saying out loud.

"I brought you a little something," he said, eyes gleaming in the moonlight.

"I know." She pointed her fork at the daisies she'd carried outside and placed in the center of the table. "I love them."

He shook his head. "I don't mean the flowers. This isn't technically a gift, just something I ran across in one of the boxes I brought with me from Austin."

He unsnapped one of the front pockets of his Western shirt, removed a photograph and slid it across the table toward her.

Susannah gasped. "Is that...me?"

She picked up the faded Polaroid and inspected it. Her fourteen-year-old self gazed back at her, barefoot on the dusty path that led to the creek. Her hair was a damp tangle from swimming all day, and she was dressed in a faded tank top and shorts. A pair of flip-flops dangled from her fingers and a dog-eared Agatha Christie novel was tucked under her arm.

"It sure is." Oliver grinned. "Do you notice the book?"

Susannah's lips twitched with amusement. "*And Then There Were None*. After I read all those Nancy Drew books that summer, the concierge at the resort introduced me to Agatha Christie."

"Like you said earlier—here we are, chasing after the desires of our hearts. I always knew you'd be a mystery writer someday." He held her gaze just long enough to make her blush.

She set the photo down on the table and toyed with the edges, softened from time. "I can't believe you still have this."

"It was tucked away with some of my other childhood mementos. I grabbed the box when I left Austin because I thought some of the old pictures and documents might help with the search for my mother's past." He flashed her a slow grin that melted her insides. "After I ran into you yesterday, I dug it back out because I remembered coming across the picture when I sorted through everything after I first got to Emerald Ridge."

"This definitely deserves a spot in my inspiration notebook." Susannah had a whole journal filled with inspirational quotes, character sketches and ideas for her manuscript. "Can I keep it?"

"Of course." Oliver arched a single, mischievous eyebrow. "So long as you keep your promise and let me read your book."

"Oh, so this isn't actually a gift. It's a *bribe*," she said, but couldn't help the laugh that bubbled out of her.

He shrugged. "A promise is a promise."

She took a deep breath. Why did the thought of Oliver reading her novel suddenly make her feel even more exposed than the first time he'd seen her altered face? "Fine. I have a fresh copy of it printed out, and I'll give it to you before you go home."

Oliver glanced at the dogs sprawled on the porch's wooden planks—Hershey stretched lazily on his side, Honey curled into a snug little circle and Bear, whose velvety ears flicked at every small sound. "Did you hear that, guys? Y'all are my witnesses."

Susannah rolled her eyes. "You're ridiculous."

He was also kind of wonderful, which was more than a little terrifying.

"Did you know that Agatha Christie once vanished for eleven days without a trace?" she asked, steering the conversation to safer territory.

A flicker of surprise crossed Oliver's face. "She did?"

Susannah nodded. "There was a huge manhunt. Her

car was found abandoned shortly after she disappeared. Then, eleven days later, authorities found her in a hotel a couple hundred miles away from her home. She'd checked in under the surname of her husband's mistress, and claimed to have lost her memory."

Oliver's eyebrows crept closer to his hairline. "That sounds like something out of one of her books."

"I know, right?" She took another sip of her wine. "Years later, she wrote an autobiography and didn't explain a thing. The whole event is still a real-life mystery."

A mystery to *others*, maybe. Susannah understood. Life had become too much for Agatha. Her mother had passed away a few months prior, and learning her husband was deeply involved with another woman had probably been the icing on the cake. In a way, Susannah had followed in her favorite author's footsteps and done the exact same thing. She'd hidden herself from the outside world.

Susannah had been doing it a lot longer than eleven days, though. And she still didn't feel ready to venture out into the world. She wasn't sure she ever could. How much longer would Agatha Christie have stayed at that hotel if someone hadn't recognized her as the missing mystery author and called the police?

"I guess everyone has their demons," Oliver said quietly, looking pensive.

Susannah nodded. "Even famous novelists."

"Even us." His smile was thoughtful, and just a little bit sad. "Sometimes I feel like my entire life has been a lie. I still love my mother, but I wish she would've told me the truth."

"I know your mother loved you, but you have every right to feel conflicted. Anyone would," she told him as gently as she could manage.

"I'm the illegitimate son of a man who had three wives, and my mom blackmailed him for millions not to expose his secret." Oliver released a sharp breath. "I think learning the truth the way I did was the biggest blow, though. I'm still reeling a bit from all of it."

"You got together with your siblings this morning to talk about Archibald's journal, right?" Susannah hadn't wanted to pry, but now that he was opening up again about his family situation, she had to find a way to show him that she cared. More than anything, she wanted to give him the same sort of emotional support he was giving her. "Was that difficult?"

Oliver's brow furrowed. "No, not really. I want a relationship with the Fortunes—all of them. But I still feel guarded around them. I wish I didn't, but I just can't help it. I had a loving, doting mom, and even she kept secrets from me. Now I keep wondering what everyone else is hiding. Can you really ever truly know a person?"

"It's official—you and I are a mess," Susannah said with a soft laugh. "But you don't have to worry about secrets with me. What you see is what you get, scars and all."

"I want to believe that," he said quietly. "But lately, trusting anyone feels like stepping onto thin ice."

She felt awful for everything Oliver was going

through, but at the same time, it made her feel more connected to him. Both of their lives had been up-ended in completely unexpected ways. Was it possible their mutual heartache just might bring them closer together?

Susannah took a deep breath. She was getting ahead of herself. They'd kissed, that's all. It didn't necessarily mean anything. They weren't a couple, for goodness' sake.

She swallowed hard, remembering a time when she didn't second-guess everything she said or did. Had it been so long since she'd had someone to talk to that she'd forgotten how to have a regular conversation?

"This is nice, Oliver."

She toyed with the stem of her wineglass, wanting to explain that yes, she'd been lonely. But tonight meant something to her. It was special because *he* was special, not just because she was desperate for human companionship.

"As I'm sure you've probably guessed, I haven't done anything like this in a long time," she continued. "I don't really talk to anyone else or even go on social media anymore. The past year has been hard, and it's been lonely at times, but I also feel like I'm slowly finding myself…or getting back to myself, rather." She averted her eyes for a moment before looking back up at him again. "For a while, I think I got so wrapped up in my career that I forgot who I really was and what I want most out of life. Sometimes, I think the accident might've been a blessing in disguise, even if I'm not fully comfortable with the person I'm becoming quite yet."

Oliver took her hand. Candlelight flickered in his soft gaze as he ran a thumb over her knuckles in slow, tender circles. "If your accident is what brought you back to my life, then I definitely consider it a blessing in disguise. But I hope you know I am so sorry about the pain it's caused you, both physically and emotionally."

Susannah's smile went watery. She did *not* want to cry. She'd shed enough tears for a lifetime over the past twelve months, and honestly thought those days were over.

But Oliver had just given her something that Brett never had—an apology. What happened wasn't Oliver's fault. He hadn't been anywhere near the Mercedes when it crashed through a guardrail and tumbled down the side of a cliff. Brett had, though. He'd been the one behind the wheel, and by some strange twist of fate, he'd walked away completely unscathed.

Then he'd kept on walking straight out of her life.

And in all that time, he'd never once told her he was sorry—for any of it. In the days immediately following the crash, Susannah assured him over and over again that everything was okay. Her biggest worry was that he would blame himself for what happened. But never in her wildest dreams had she imagined that the man she loved would look at her through cold, unrecognizable eyes and tell her he didn't think they could make it work now that she'd changed, inside and out.

He hadn't just left…he'd *gutted* her first. As if the

accident had changed not only her face but her soul. Like surviving had somehow made her less.

The irony was, even back then, in some small, painful way, he'd been right—she wasn't the same. How could she be? She'd seen death up close, had come back from the edge with shattered bones and a face she hardly recognized. But what Brett never understood, what he never stayed long enough to see, was that she'd become stronger. Quieter, maybe. More guarded…definitely. But not broken, nor ruined.

Still, those words had taken root. They'd grown wild inside her over the months, like ivy crawling over a house abandoned in a storm. She'd built walls around herself and called it survival.

But Oliver…

He hadn't pretended not to see the scars. He didn't just tell her she was still beautiful, but he *showed* her that she was still whole by the way he looked at her, steady and unflinching. When she saw herself through his eyes, she didn't feel broken anymore. She felt free. And now he was saying the words that Brett had never had the courage to utter.

I am so sorry.

Those words cracked something open in her, something she'd thought long since buried under the rubble of that crash and everything that followed.

"Please don't cry, honey." Oliver reached to brush a tear from her cheek, and for once, she forgot to flinch at the thought of someone touching her scar. "I didn't mean to upset you. We don't have to talk about the accident if you're not ready."

"You didn't upset me. It's just…" She let out a shaky breath and searched for the right words, ones that wouldn't make her sound fragile or foolish. "No one has ever told me they were sorry for what I've been through. It means a lot. I don't think I realized how badly I needed to hear it."

His gaze sharpened, and she knew he probably had questions about Brett. She didn't blame him, and she'd tell him whatever he wanted to know—later. Tonight had been so lovely, and she didn't want to ruin things by talking about her ex-fiancé. The past would still be there tomorrow, and if Oliver wanted to know, she'd tell him every piece of it. But not now when the stars were beginning to spill across the sky and his hand was wrapped around hers like she was worth holding on to.

"Enough about that for now. Tell me more about your land next door and all your big plans." She squeezed his hand, anchoring them to the present. "I want to know everything."

The corner of his mouth tipped up in a boyish way that made her chest flutter. "How about I do you one better and show you instead of just talking about it? I can take you on a tour tomorrow if you don't have plans."

Plans? Susannah couldn't remember the last time she'd jotted anything down in her calendar that didn't involve a doctor's appointment or recovery milestone. "I think I can pencil you in between dog walks and sipping sweet tea out here in one of the rocking chairs."

"Busy woman," he said with a smile that reached

all the way to his rich brown eyes. "I'll try not to slow you down."

He lifted his wine to seal their plans with a toast, and their fingertips brushed as she clinked her glass against it. A tranquil stillness settled between them.

"Is morning okay?" he asked, his voice a little quieter now.

She nodded, her smile curling with something she couldn't quite contain. "I'll be here."

His gaze lingered on hers, and even though Susannah told herself not to get carried away, the moment brimmed with promise.

"Then so will I."

Chapter Six

After Oliver left Susannah's ranch and returned to his room at the Emerald Ridge Hotel, he tossed his Stetson aside and started reading her manuscript. It was already late, but curiosity got the best of him. He couldn't wait to dive in.

A few pages later, he ordered a cup of coffee from room service. *Just one more chapter, and then I'll hit the hay.* Three chapters later, he caved and ordered an entire pot.

Susannah had undersold herself. She was a talented storyteller. Oliver simply couldn't put the book down. It was hard to believe the freshly printed pages she'd handed him—practically under duress—represented her very first attempt at writing. On the other hand, he wasn't surprised in the slightest. The girl he'd known back when they were kids had been born to write mysteries. It had been in her blood. After she'd devoured all of those Nancy Drew books from the resort library, Susannah declared she wanted to be Carolyn Keene when she grew up. A few days later, after she'd found out the name was merely a pseudonym for a number of authors who all contributed to the series, she'd *cried.*

Was it any wonder that someone with that kind of passion for the mysteries she loved so much would be able to craft one of her own that could keep him so riveted?

Oliver glanced up from the pages, momentarily disoriented by how real it all felt—the tension, the clues, the small-town characters who somehow felt like real people. It was Susannah's voice on the page. He could hear her reading the words aloud as clear as if she'd been sitting right beside him on the hotel bed. Still, it felt like she was telling him about an actual murder, not a fictional story.

He looked down at the manuscript again, and before he knew it, he was lost in the narrative again, deciphering clues and trying to work out the ending—which, as it turned out, he never saw coming. Then he sat for a long moment, his thumb trailing over the margin where she'd scribbled a nervous apology in pencil.

This probably isn't any good. I just wanted to see if I could finish something.

Oliver shook his head slowly, affection settling deep in his chest. Susannah hadn't just finished something. She'd *started* something. Her movie career had been overwhelmingly successful. That was an indisputable fact. But if what she said was true and her time in Hollywood had made her lose track of what she really wanted out of life, then being a film star had never truly made her happy. He couldn't imagine why she'd chased that dream in the first place. She was meant to be a writer. Oliver knew it as surely as he knew his own name.

He snorted to himself. What *was* his name, again?

It had changed enough times that he was beginning to lose track.

That thought gave him pause. He kept thinking Susannah was the same person she'd been over a decade ago, but how did he really know that was true? People changed. Even his own mother had hidden her true self from him, and Oliver had been too blindly devoted to her to question it, despite all the red flags. He couldn't trust his judgment anymore, and here he was, already emotionally wrapped up in a woman whose entire career involved pretending to be somebody else. She was a highly celebrated actress, famous for her ability to embody other people, for crying out loud. If Oliver was smart, he'd take a step back and put some distance between them before somebody got hurt.

But it was too late for that.

He was already on the verge of falling. Again. And the stack of paper in his hands only sealed the deal. This wasn't acting. It was authentically Susannah. And whether or not he could trust his judgment, his heart was already tangled up like a calf caught in a lasso.

"Good morning." Susannah regarded him with a tilt of her head the next day as he made his way from the meandering trail that straddled their property lines and stepped up onto her back porch. "Is it my imagination or do you look tired?"

"I didn't get much sleep last night," he said, squatting to pet the dogs.

The trio of Labs bounded toward him the moment his boots hit the porch's wooden planks, ears flapping and tails whipping back and forth. Hershey reached him first, shoving his nose under Oliver's hand with a huff, demanding affection. Honey circled twice before leaning against him with a groan of pleasure, while Bear pawed at him, whining softly like he hadn't just seen him the night before.

"Good morning to y'all, too," Oliver chuckled, letting himself get swarmed.

He'd found Susannah exactly where she'd said she would be—moving gently in one of the rocking chairs that overlooked a towering pecan tree, a glass of sweet tea in her hand. A pitcher sat on the low table in front of her with an empty glass and a plate of freshly sliced lemons beside it.

"Why couldn't you sleep?" A frown tugged at the corners of Susannah's pillowy lips. If Oliver hadn't stayed up half the night reading her manuscript, he probably would've spent that time lying awake thinking about kissing that lush mouth of hers again. So it was a wash, really. "Between your family stuff and deciding what to do with your ranch, you've got a lot going on. Was your mind too busy running in circles to get some rest?"

"Something like that." He grinned at her.

She narrowed her gaze at him. "Something like that?"

He settled into the rocking chair beside hers. It let out a soft creak as he rocked to and fro. "I read your manuscript last night."

Susannah's eyes lit up. "You mean you started it?"

"Nope." He rocked back a little farther, drawing it out just to see her squirm. "I finished it."

She gasped. "You *didn't*."

"I sure did, and I have the bags under my eyes to prove it." He winked at her. "Isn't that what you just said?"

"I didn't mean it like that." Her cheeks went pink. With her wind-tossed blond hair, fresh-scrubbed face and long eyelet skirt paired with well-worn cowboy boots, she looked as carefree as he'd seen her since they'd become reacquainted. It was nice to see her happy like this, and even nicer to think he might be the reason she'd started to relax a bit.

"I'm just teasing you, Suzy Q. If I look tired, you're fully responsible. I couldn't put your book down," he said.

"Seriously?"

"Seriously. It's good, sweetheart." The endearment slipped out before he could stop it. "*Really* good."

She looked at him askance, even as her grin widened until it lit up her entire face. "You're not just saying that to make me feel good, are you?"

"I couldn't lie to you if I tried. Need I remind you that only one of us has been nominated for an Oscar, and it wasn't me?" He lifted an eyebrow.

She laughed, and before he realized what she was doing, she moved over to his rocker and sat down on his lap. Then she removed his Stetson, plopped it down on her own head and gave him a gentle kiss on the cheek.

"Thank you," she whispered, and her breath brushed

warm against his skin. "Your opinion on this means more to me than just about anyone else's."

"Careful there. If you keep that up, I might start to think you're sweet on me," he teased.

She leaned back just enough for her eyes to meet his and returned his gaze with a tenderness that nearly undid him.

"Maybe I am."

Susannah hadn't been horseback riding in years. But it all came back to her as easily as breathing—the gentle sway of the horse beneath her, the quiet thud of hooves on soft earth, the familiar give and stretch of the reins in her hands.

It probably helped that Oliver had arranged to borrow two of his sister Shelby's gentlest horses from Fortune and Daughters Ranch. Susannah had a feeling he'd arranged to show her his land on horseback because of her limp, but she didn't feel the usual embarrassment about her physical challenges. She was too caught up in the simple wonder of riding again. Her heart had leaped in her chest when she caught her first glimpse of the sweet horses. Oliver had hinted at a surprise and said she might want to leave Hershey, Honey and Bear at home. Once she'd gotten the dogs settled back in the log house, she and Oliver walked the path back to his side of the property line, hand in hand. He gave her palm a light squeeze just as the trail spilled out from the wooded area, and there they were—a buttery-blond palomino and a glossy chestnut mare tied to a towering oak tree, all saddled up and ready to go.

Oliver introduced the horses as Butterscotch and Dulce, and then let her choose which one she wanted to ride. She picked Butterscotch, of course.

"We blondes have to stick together, don't we?" she said as she ran her fingers through the palomino's sun-warmed mane.

The horse answered with a welcoming nicker, and when Susannah reached out to touch her again, Butterscotch leaned in gently, pressing her velvety-soft muzzle against Susannah's palm. They'd become instant friends.

Oliver led the way, and they set off at a leisurely pace, riding side by side along a trail that curved around the tree line. The morning sun streamed through the spindly branches of the oak trees, dappling the path in gold and amber. With each clip-clop of Butterscotch's hooves, Susannah felt herself relax more and more. Then she realized why it felt so nice to ride again—she didn't have to worry about her limp while she was on horseback. She could move about as freely and easily as she had before the accident.

It had taken months of physical therapy to regain the use of her injured leg, and the fact that she could walk at all was its own triumph. Susannah was as grateful for her mobility as she was her life. Not many people survived driving off a cliff, Brett's freakishly good luck notwithstanding. But being able to move like this without holding her breath at each slight incline or gripping her walking stick for dear life every time the path got a little rocky was freeing in a way she hadn't anticipated. It made her feel like…she could do anything.

With just the slightest press of one of her thighs, the horse would shift left or right. Susannah hardly needed the reins. The mare seemed to sense when to stop and when to go, when to trot or canter and when to slow to a gentle, four-beat walk.

Susannah patted Butterscotch's thick neck, hoping the horse could somehow sense her appreciation. The palomino's muscles flexed beneath her fingers and she let out a soft whinny.

Oliver slid them a sideways glance, eyes crinkling near the corners. "Everything okay over there? How are my two favorite blondes getting along?"

"We're best friends now." She stroked Butterscotch's mane again. It was surprisingly soft and silky. "Just don't tell Hershey, Honey and Bear."

Oliver winked at her. "Your secrets are always safe with me."

With Butterscotch's shoulder lined up just near Dulce's flank, Susannah had a nice, clear view of Oliver situated in the saddle. He moved perfectly in sync with Dulce, as if he and the horse were one. With his trademark Stetson and boots that looked like they'd seen their fair share of rodeos, Oliver looked every inch the cowboy. It was his peaceful expression that really hit her square in the feels, though. He seemed as happy and relaxed as she'd seen him since they'd become reacquainted—like the boy she remembered who'd dreamed of being a cowboy someday, complete with cattle drives and camping out at night under the stars.

"I thought we'd take a loop around the north pasture," he said, pulling the brim of his hat down just a bit. "There's something I want to show you."

Susannah nodded, adjusting her hold on the reins. "Lead the way, cowboy."

They rode in comfortable silence for a while until the land gradually opened up, revealing rolling hills dotted with wildflowers and brush, a shallow stream snaking its way along the edge of the field. Oliver pointed to a wide, flat stretch of earth shaded by a cluster of cottonwoods.

"I'm thinking this spot here for the cattle barn," he said. "A nice, roomy one with space for stalls, feed, maybe even an office."

Susannah turned in the saddle to take it in. "It's perfect," she murmured. "Level, shaded. Close to water."

He nodded, then pointed out toward a low rise in the distance. "I imagine the cattle grazing up on that ridge. There's plenty of space to rotate them through. And near the riverbank, there's a good place for a tack shed and maybe a little cabin for ranch hands down the line."

She glanced at him, curious. "You've really been thinking this through."

"I have," he confirmed, his voice lower now, gravelly with an intimacy that sent a shiver up and down Susannah's spine. "Last night...talking with you, something clicked. I've been straddling two worlds since discovering I'm a Fortune. The Austin place has been good to me for a long time, but it's not where my heart is anymore."

He guided Dulce to a stop on a gentle slope that

overlooked the property. Butterscotch slowed alongside, her ears flicking in the breeze.

"I called a Realtor this morning to officially put the Austin ranch on the market, and I'm meeting with an architect down here who specializes in ranch design. Madeline's fiancé, Forrest, is a ranchland developer, and he's offered to help in any way he can. I'm ready to go all in and make this spot right here mine. I want to raise cattle and horses right here." He swept the horizon with his gaze as he cleared his throat. "It only seems fitting…maybe even fated."

Susannah's breath caught as she looked out over the expanse of his inherited land. There was a hush to the place, like it had been holding its breath, waiting for another Fortune to truly call it home.

"I think you're right," she whispered. "About the fate part."

They sat for a moment in silence, just watching the wind move through the grass, the horses shifting their weight beneath them. Butterscotch gave a soft snort, and Dulce flicked her tail lazily.

Susannah reached across the space between them and touched Oliver's hand. "Your family land deserves someone who will pour their heart into it."

He gave her a look filled with so much tenderness that she felt it all the way down to her toes. "So do you, you know."

Her pulse raced so fast she could hear it echoing in her ears. What were they doing? Neither of them was in a place to start something real, something *permanent*. She'd told herself this a million times over the past few days. But out here on the land where Oliver's father and grandparents had experienced so much pain and heartbreak, she couldn't quite remember the reasons why it was such a bad idea.

"Let's go." Oliver made a clicking sound with his tongue and Dulce shifted to a more alert posture and took a step. Butterscotch followed suit. "Your surprise is just around the bend."

Another surprise, besides the horses? When he'd said he wanted to show her something, she'd thought this was it—the land itself and the spot where he wanted to build. But after a minute or two, they reached a small clearing nestled between a ring of old oak trees. Oliver gently tugged the reins and dismounted in one easy motion. Butterscotch halted too, as if sensing the moment—standing perfectly still, waiting for Susannah to do the same.

"I've got you," Oliver said.

He helped brace her bad leg as she swung the other one over Butterscotch's back, stumbling only slightly as she landed beside him. She was about to ask where they were when she noticed the red-and-white-checkered blanket spread beneath one of the trees, anchored in place by a large wicker picnic basket. A folded quilt sat atop it, tucked beside a silver metal tub overflowing with ice and cool bottles of root beer.

Susannah's hand flew to her chest. "You did this?"

Oliver gave a small shrug, eyes lowering beneath the brim of his hat. "I thought after the ride, you might like to rest a bit. And I remembered you said you used to love picnics with your grandma."

Her throat tightened. It had been *years* since any-one had remembered something like that. Had she ever even mentioned those picnics to Brett?

She didn't think so. It was strange how something that had once been so important to her had faded into the background of her memories, outshone by the razzle-dazzle of life on center stage. That was the thing about spotlights, though. They shone so bright that they over-whelmed your senses and made it near impossible to see anything else. Now that Susannah had stepped away from Hollywood, everything she'd neglected or given up on her rise to fame was coming back with crystal clear focus.

What had all that sacrifice been for anyway? She'd become a completely different person, all for a life that was so shallow that it had disappeared in the blink of an eye.

A flush of shame radiated through her chest. She didn't deserve such kindness from Oliver, or at least Susannah Simmons the movie star didn't.

"Thank you. This is so lovely and so…" She forced a smile. He still saw her as Suzy, and she ached to be that girl again. "…unexpected."

They sat down together on the blanket, the horses grazing quietly nearby. Oliver opened the basket to reveal sandwiches, cut fruit and a large slice of lemon cake wrapped in wax paper.

"You thought of everything," she said, unwrapping a sandwich—pimento cheese, her favorite.

She looked down, her appetite suddenly forgotten. It had been such a long time since she'd felt this kind of care. Uncomplicated. Earnest. *Sincere.* It meant more to her than any of the lavish gifts that had been bestowed on her in recent years. Those luxuries had always come at some unseen cost, whether it was a fake smile for the cameras, a dinner she didn't really want to attend or a version of herself she had to perform. Even the things Brett had given her had come with strings. She just hadn't realized it at the time.

It was the simple, heartfelt kindnesses like today that were going to be her undoing. The horseback riding, the picnic, staying up all night to read her manuscript... Slowly but surely, Oliver was making her feel like she was a woman worth romancing. Maybe even a woman worth loving, no matter what kind of mistakes or bad choices she'd made or whom or what she'd lost along the way.

She was falling harder and faster than she meant to. Faster than she *wanted* to. And it scared the heck out of her. The next time she gave her heart away—if there ever was a next time—she needed to know without a doubt that she was giving it to the right man, for all the right reasons. Love wasn't meant to fill a void or to silence the doubts that told her she was unworthy or too broken to matter. She needed to know she'd found acceptance in her own eyes first. Not in a man's and not in the public's view of her.

Was she ready? Had she found that kind of peace yet?

A bite of sandwich lodged in her throat as Oliver stretched out beside her, one hand tucked under his head, the other resting between them on the blanket.

His fingertips brushed hers—just barely, just enough to send her heart fluttering.

She looked at him. *Really looked.* He had hat hair from his Stetson, which was now resting on the quilt. Laugh lines framed his eyes, and weariness lingered on his face, either from lack of sleep or all the turmoil in his personal life. None of that mattered, though. He was still the most handsome man she'd ever set eyes on—yesterday, today, always. He wasn't trying to impress her, and he didn't want or need anything from her. He just *cared.*

Oliver turned his head to look at her, a slow, affectionate smile tugging at his lips, and Susannah felt a shift deep inside her. This man she'd known and cared about for more than half her life was helping her find her way back to herself. And no matter how hard she tried not to…

She just might love him for it.

Chapter Seven

Oliver spent the next few days, from sunup to sundown, sorting out the logistics of transforming his newly inherited property into a working cattle ranch. There were real estate documents to sign, contractors to hire and a hundred decisions to make—each one weighed down by his determination to do the right thing and honor the Fortune legacy. Archibald had made his fair share of mistakes, and Oliver knew it was neither his place nor responsibility to right them, but he wanted the ranch to represent a new beginning.

A healing, of sorts. Not just for him, but for all the Fortunes, too.

In addition to the business side of things, Oliver spent his days tackling the physical work his new land required—clearing brush, repairing old fencing, digging postholes, and hauling lumber for the small barn he planned to build before winter. By the time the sun dipped behind the hills, his muscles ached in places he hadn't known existed. He was exhausted...

And happier than he'd been in years.

He was getting a taste of what he wanted—an authentic life centered on respect for the land and his animals. And he loved every minute of it.

Oliver tipped his hat at the front desk clerk at the Emerald Ridge Hotel as he strode through the pristine lobby after mending the fence surrounding the back acre. Life would get simpler once he had somewhere to sleep on the ranch. It would also get sweeter, because he'd be closer to Susannah.

Oliver's phone rang as he approached the elevator bank, and he slipped it from the back pocket of his Wranglers, hoping to see her name on the display screen. He hadn't seen her since their picnic a few days ago, but he called her every night when he got back to the hotel and they kept up a constant stream of text messages throughout the day. Sometimes he felt like a goofy teenager, constantly checking his phone and grinning like an idiot. Then he'd remind himself that they weren't kids anymore, and this wasn't a summer vacation. This was real adult life, and it was complicated and messy.

He and Susannah were just old friends…

Friends who held hands, kissed occasionally and couldn't seem to go to bed without telling each other good-night, but *just friends*. Still, he couldn't shake the feeling that something real had sparked between them, even if the timing was less than ideal. And now, every time his phone buzzed, his chest filled with hope before he could stop it.

It wasn't her name that scrolled across the display screen, though. Not this time.

"Hey, Forrest," Oliver said as he held the phone up

to his ear, stepping into the elevator and jabbing the button for his floor.

Forrest and Madeline met a few months ago when she purchased a plot of land in Emerald Ridge to build a miniature version of Cowboy Country USA amusement park for Kate Fortune's upcoming one-hundredth birthday party. Forrest was a single dad to twin toddler daughters. Like Oliver, the man had a lot on his plate, which only made it more meaningful that he'd offered to help with the designs for the inherited land.

"Hey, man," said Forrest. "I hope this isn't a bad time."

"Not at all." The elevator doors swished open and Oliver made his way down the hall, wondering what his sister's fiancé might want. "Shoot."

"Great. I'm arranging a little surprise, and I'm trying to sneak phone calls to everyone while Madeline isn't around."

"A surprise?" Oliver asked as he swiped his card key.

"Yeah. The twins have started toddler preschool, and I want to have a little celebration. I know your sister is a professional party planner and would do a much better job than I will, but she's been such a positive influence on my girls. This celebration is for her, too. Madeline never gets to just enjoy these types of things because she's always the one putting them together," Forrest said.

Oliver felt himself smile. "Hence the surprise."

"Hence the surprise," Forrest echoed with a chuckle. "The party is this Saturday, and I'd love it if you could be there. Nothing fancy. It's an intimate family gathering. I'm inviting all the Fortunes, obviously. Along with their significant others."

There was a pause, because as they both knew, Oliver was the only sibling who hadn't found love in Emerald Ridge. Not that he was looking or anything.

He cleared his throat and tried not to think about Susannah. Oliver still had zero confidence in his ability to read people. *Thanks for that, Mom and Dad.* Was she really in Texas to stay, or would she go running back to Hollywood once she'd regained her confidence? He wanted to believe her when she said that all she wanted now was a normal life, but he knew she'd been hurt.

Not just physically, but emotionally, too.

She was healing now. He could see it, and every little step she made tugged at his heartstrings. Oliver was rooting for her 1,000 percent, no matter what that healing looked like. That said, recent events had turned him into a realist. Emerald Ridge might not be as permanent as she thought it was once she finally came all the way out of her shell.

"I'll be there. Thanks for the invitation," Oliver said, and then the words were out of his mouth before he could stop them. "I'd like to bring a date, if that's okay?"

"A date? Sure, of course. Sorry, I didn't know you were seeing anyone."

"It's Susannah Simmons. We're…" Oliver tossed his Stetson on the bed and dragged a hand through his hair "…old friends."

The second the words were out of his mouth, it felt

like a lie. Did he really think he could outsmart his own feelings?

"Madeline mentioned you knew her. I just didn't realize you two were so close," Forrest said, and Oliver could hear the smile in his voice. "*Definitely* bring her. My beautiful fiancée would come unglued if she got to meet Susannah in person and talk to her about Kate's party."

"I'd like to invite her, but honestly, I'm not sure she'll come. She's…shy." Oliver figured he didn't need to elaborate since her accident and withdrawal from public life had been literal front-page news.

"Well, we'd love to have her," Forrest reiterated, and then he gave Oliver the necessary party details.

He jotted them down on the hotel notepad. From what Forrest described, it was going to be a small, low-key family affair. Kids, cupcakes, party streamers. It might be the perfect setting for Susannah to dip her toe back into the world.

More than that, Oliver just wanted her there. It would thrill him to see her relaxed and happy around other people. And deep down, he wanted his newfound family to know her.

He picked up the phone again and tapped Susannah's contact information, palms sweating like he was inviting her to prom instead of a toddler surprise party. She answered on the first ring.

"Hi there, cowboy." It was her usual greeting, which Oliver liked far more than he cared to think about.

"Hi there, Nancy Drew."

They talked for a few minutes about her manuscript,

which she'd sent to a literary agent she'd met once at a Hollywood party. The agent had kept in touch, suggesting that Susannah should write a memoir. She wasn't sure if the agent would be interested in a fiction book, but she was giving it a shot.

"That's great. I'm really proud of you for putting yourself out there like that." Oliver knew it was no small thing. She could write, though. He had a feeling she could have a whole new career as a mystery author...

If that's what she wanted.

"We'll see what happens. Baby steps, right?" She laughed, and Oliver could hear one of the dogs playing with a squeak toy in the background. "I'm excited, though. There's something comforting about feeling hopeful again. I've missed it."

And that was Oliver's cue to mention the toddler party. "In that case, maybe I've got a little something else you can look forward to. Nothing major, I promise. Madeline's fiancé is throwing a surprise family get-together. I'd love it if you came with me."

The phone line went instantly quiet.

"As my date," he added.

She didn't respond right away, and he could practically hear her thoughts racing on the other end.

"I just thought it might be nice. It's going to be a simple, low-key afternoon with people who care—cupcakes, finger paint and you and me showing up together." He swallowed. "No pressure, though. I'll understand if you'd rather not come."

She took a deep breath, and he could hear the hitch

in it, the hesitation. "You're just full of surprises, aren't you?"

The memory of their picnic tugged at him—Susannah looking so peaceful and content in the saddle, her long, beautiful hair fanned out over the red-checkered blanket, her warm lips pressed against his, tasting tart and sweet, like lemon cake.

"What can I say? I like a surprise. Big fan of them, actually," he teased.

"Okay, then," she said in a voice so quiet that he almost didn't hear her.

"Okay?" His heart did a ridiculous flip in his chest. "Does that mean what I think it means?"

She laughed. "It means okay… I'd like to go. I think so, at least. I'll admit it's a little daunting to consider, but I'd love to meet your siblings. I've heard so much about them, and it will be great to put some faces with the various names. Venturing out might actually be fun."

Honey barked, and then resumed squeaking her dog toy with renewed vigor. Oliver heard the scramble of Labrador paws on the log home's hardwood floors and could only imagine the canine antics that were going on over there.

"Would it be less daunting if we brought Hershey, Honey and Bear to the party, too?"

"Are you sure?" she asked. "Bringing three large dogs along seems like an awfully big ask."

"The party is outdoors on Forrest's ranch. The dogs would have loads of room to run and play, plus I know the twins would love them," Oliver said. He'd run the idea past Forrest first, of course, but he couldn't imagine it would be a problem.

"They're pretty great with kids." Susannah still didn't sound convinced, though.

"Let me talk to Forrest about it. I just know how much emotional support your canine crew gives you, and I think you'll feel less anxious with them by your side."

"You're right about that part," she said, and he could hear a quaver of uncertainty in her voice. It was faint, but very much there. "I just don't want to be a bother. I'll probably be a big enough sideshow as it is."

"You wouldn't be a bother," he countered. "Not even a little. I promise."

There was another brief pause, filled only by the jingle of dog tags. Hershey, no doubt. All of Susannah's dogs were loyal, but the chocolate Lab was the one who always seemed to know when she needed a little extra comfort and support.

"If Forrest truly doesn't mind, then yes, all four of us would love to attend," she murmured, and for the first time, she sounded like she might actually be looking forward to it.

Relief bloomed in Oliver's chest. "See you Saturday, then."

"It's a date," she said with just enough tender optimism in her tone to make him believe she'd actually go through with it.

Hope, it seemed, was catching.

What was I thinking, accepting Oliver's invitation? Susannah stared at her reflection in the mirror Saturday morning, doing her best to fend off a panic attack.

Venturing into town in a disguise was one thing. But attending an actual social event? That was another matter entirely. Oliver had tried to downplay it as an intimate family gathering, but the Fortunes were a huge family. He had *five* siblings, for goodness' sake. How intimate could it possibly be?

"That's it." She set her brush down on the bathroom vanity. She'd tried every hairstyle in the book already, hoping for a miracle. Unfortunately, a pretty, flattering style that simultaneously hid half of her face didn't seem to exist. "I'm not going."

Hershey, who'd been sitting beside her and watching her numerous failed attempts at a half updo with rapt interest, rested his head on her thigh and let out a quiet woof.

"What?" Susannah frowned down at the chocolate Lab. "Don't judge me. You're not the one who's going to be walking into a party while everyone stares."

Except Hershey would be there, thanks to Oliver. Forrest loved the idea of bringing the dogs along to the surprise party, so Honey and Bear would be there, too. In all her time in show business, Susannah had never witnessed a scene-stealer quite as effective as her trio of Labradors. Maybe everyone would be too busy looking at them to notice the scarred, has-been movie star at the other end of their leashes.

She closed her eyes and took a deep breath. She'd always found comfort in the gentle pressure of a dog leaning against her or a warm muzzle pressed to her thigh. After she'd adopted her Labradors, she'd immediately ordered a stack of books about dogs, training and the human-animal bond. One of the paperbacks had devoted an entire chapter to deep-pressure therapy, in which the author compared the calming effect of a dog's body weight to the sensation of a weighted blanket. Susannah got it. It worked, and as far as canine deep-pressure therapists went, Hershey was a master.

She opened her eyes and sighed. "Fine, you win."

The dog was right. She'd promised Oliver she would be there, and while she knew he'd understand if she changed her mind, the joy in his tone when she'd agreed to be his date for the party had been unmistakable. She'd feel awful backing out at the last minute.

Susannah picked up the brush again. "Back to the drawing board…"

In the end, she decided on a simple low ponytail, paired with a wide-brimmed sun hat and the darkest pair of large-framed, prescription-free sunglasses in her arsenal. At least they would be appropriate since the surprise party was taking place outdoors. Oliver had mentioned a bubble machine, kiddie pools and a petting zoo where the children could interact with baby goats and lambs that Forrest had procured from a local farmer friend. He'd also arranged for a few Shetlands to be on hand for pony rides. Madeline might be the party planner in the relationship, but it sounded like Forrest was really going all out.

Oliver picked her up right on time, and Hershey, Honey and Bear piled into the back of his luxury SUV while Susannah sat beside him in the front seat. The bouquet of flowers she'd picked from her garden rested on the console between them, tied with a pink satin bow and a card for Madeline. She'd also gotten matching white cowgirl hats for the twins, decorated with sparkly sequined stars.

"I hope you didn't feel pressured to bring gifts," Oliver said as he navigated through downtown Emerald Ridge. "It was really thoughtful of you, though."

"Oh, it was no trouble. I enjoyed picking something out for the girls. Who knew there were so many cute Texas-themed ideas for twin toddlers?" Susannah mused.

He glanced over at her and smiled, and she tried not to think about having children with this kind, generous man someday. She could see it all as clear as day in her imagination—pony rides on the land where Oliver's father and grandparents had once lived, teaching her little girl how to roll out dough for piecrust in the kitchen at the big log house in the woods, a baby boy dressed in overalls with eyes as warm and brown as his daddy's. Her throat closed up tight at the mere idea of it.

"Everything okay? Are you still with me?" Oliver flashed her a wink as the vehicle crawled past the gates of Forrest's ranch.

"Peachy." Susannah pasted on a smile and pretended she hadn't just mapped out an entire imaginary future for the two of them during their first official date. "Sorry, I guess I just have a lot on my mind."

"You've got nothing to worry about, sweetheart. I'm sure the Fortunes are going to be as welcoming to you as they've been to me." Oliver shifted the SUV into Park, and the dogs panted excitedly in unison, aware that they'd reached their destination.

"It's going to be fun." Susannah nodded, but her heart was already galloping like a runaway horse.

Here goes nothing.

She climbed out of the car and balanced herself on her walking stick as the dogs jumped down onto the gravel drive. They stood patiently while she clipped their leashes onto their collars. Then, no sooner had she adjusted the brim of her sun hat, pulling it as low as she could possibly get away with, than a group of Fortunes appeared, grinning broadly, offering hugs to her and Oliver and enthusiastic pats for the Labs.

"Susannah, this is my sister Shelby," Oliver said, gesturing to a heavily pregnant young woman with piercing hazel eyes and a lovely peaches-and-cream complexion. Maybe that whole pregnancy-glow thing wasn't just a myth, after all. "And this is my brother Hayes and sister Jillian."

He motioned to the other two adults, as well as a little girl who looked to be about four years old who stood in front of Jillian. His sister's hands were planted gently on the child's shoulders.

"Hi, Susannah. It's such a pleasure to meet you." Jillian lifted her fingertips in a flippy wave, then winced as the little girl launched herself at Hershey and threw her arms around his big, furry neck. "I hope this is okay. Mandy just adores dogs," Jillian said.

Susannah let out a soft laugh. "It's fine. All three of them are gentle giants—particularly Hershey. He's a really special boy."

She leaned against her cane to crouch down and show Mandy how to scratch the Labrador behind his ears, just the way he liked it. "If you rub his ears between your fingers like this, he'll be your friend for life."

She winked, and the child's eyes danced as she mimicked Susannah's motions and Hershey groaned with pleasure.

"His ears are soft," Mandy said in a small voice.

"They are, aren't they?" Susannah winked. "I always say they feel like velvet."

The little girl's eyes went wide and she gasped. "They do!"

"Well, Susannah. You and your dogs are officially the hit of the party, and we haven't even left the driveway yet." Hayes grinned and then hitched a thumb over his shoulder. "We should probably get back out there. Forrest wants everyone in place, ready to yell 'surprise' when Madeline gets here with the girls."

Susannah stood. Oliver's family was acting so normal around her that she was already starting to relax.

"Let's go. I can't wait to meet everyone else," she said.

And against all odds, she actually meant it.

Chapter Eight

Half an hour later, after Madeline and the twins had arrived to cheers and excited yells of "surprise," Susannah felt like an honorary Fortune.

Oliver had introduced her to his other brother, Penn—along with what felt like a steady stream of his siblings' significant others—as soon as they'd made their way to party headquarters on the lush green lawn behind Forrest's mansion. Susannah had hardly believed her eyes when she first caught sight of the party setup.

Forrest had really gone all out for the celebration. There were the pony rides Oliver had mentioned, an adorable petting zoo and hay bales for seating. A children's stick horse rodeo was already in full swing in a pop-up arena roped off with pink streamers. Kids galloped around in circles while a teenager with a sheriff's badge waved a toy pistol to start each race. The stick horses had googly eyes and yarn manes, and Susannah got the feeling Forrest had made them himself. It was all very homespun and charming, albeit on an impressive scale.

"This is kind of amazing," she'd said, unable to keep

the smile from spreading across her face as she took it all in. "I feel like I'm at the county fair, Fortunes' version."

Oliver had reacted with a chuckle and a shake of his head. "That tracks. *Subtle* isn't anywhere in the Fortunes' vocabulary."

With so much going on, it was easy for Susannah to blend right in. No one stared at her scar or her cane, and she wasn't bombarded with nosy questions, either. Why would anyone care about her dramatic sun hat when there were pygmy goats wearing party hats just ten feet away?

"Susannah, you have no idea how happy I am to meet you." Madeline embraced her like she was a long-lost friend within minutes of her arrival. "I'm so happy Oliver invited you."

Like the other Fortunes, Madeline radiated kindness. Susannah was instantly ashamed of how determined she'd been to avoid the woman now standing before her.

"I couldn't be happier to be here." Susannah glanced around. "You Fortunes really know how to throw a celebration."

"I had a feeling Forrest was up to something, but *this*." Madeline shook her head as the twins toddled past her, each one cradling a live rabbit from the petting zoo in their arms. "I didn't see any of this coming. If Forrest isn't careful, I might put him to work at Let's Get This Party Started."

"I heard that." Forrest paused to drop a kiss on his fiancée's cheek as he walked past with a tray of Cokes, the frosty bottles topped with classic red-and-white-striped straws. "No chance. Arranging this little party was no joke. I have a whole new respect for your profession."

"Speaking of your job, Forrest. Can we chat for a second about the revised site plan for the ranch?" Oliver cast him an apologetic glance. "I promise it won't take long."

"Sure thing. Come with me—we can talk and pass out drinks at the same time," Forrest said. "We can get Nick looped in, too. He's already been taking care of your land for a while and, as you know, he's got a lot of experience in ranch management. I'm sure he'll be happy to help."

Oliver turned toward Susannah. "Will you be okay here alone for a few minutes? I'll be right back."

"Go." Susannah made a shooing motion. "I'm having a great time. You don't need to babysit me."

"Besides, she's *not* alone." Madeline arched a perfectly sculpted eyebrow. "What am I? Chopped liver?"

Oliver held up his hands in a gesture of surrender. "Okay, okay! I know when I'm outnumbered."

Susannah laughed as the two men strode toward the tent that housed the pony rides, passing out bottles of Coke as they went and roping Nick, Jillian's fiancé, into their group. It was sweet of Oliver to feel protective of her, but she was glad to have a few minutes alone with Madeline.

Hershey must've picked up on her guilty conscience, because he rose from the bale of hay where he'd been keeping a watchful eye on the baby goats and came to lean against her legs. Susannah rested her hand on his smooth brown head and offered Oliver's sister a conciliatory smile. "Madeline, I want to apologize for ignoring your calls and messages about Kate Fortune's one-hundredth birthday party. I feel awful that I haven't been in contact."

"No hard feelings at all." Madeline pressed a hand to her heart. "And there's no need to apologize. Oliver explained things a little, and I completely understand. I didn't mean to pressure you. But Kate didn't leave me much choice. She *really* wants you there."

"That's what Oliver said." She furrowed her brow, puzzled. "I guess I'm just surprised. I haven't seen Kate in years."

She'd assumed her Great-Great-Aunt Kate had forgotten all about her. Which was silly, really, because the reverse certainly wasn't true. When Susannah was a little girl, her family traveled to Texas every summer to visit Kate. There'd been barbecue cookouts, homemade ice cream and Fourth of July fireworks, with everyone gathered on a patchwork quilt, fireflies blinking all around and sparklers sizzling in their hands. Aunt Kate had even been with her on the vacation to Austin where she'd first met Oliver. Susannah had come back to the cabin late one night after s'mores on the riverbank, hair damp and her head filled with dreamy thoughts about a young man's easy smile. Kate had taken one look at her and known exactly what was going on.

"Remember, darling—it's okay to have butterflies," she said with a wink. "Just don't let them carry you off."

After the falling-out between Kate and Susannah's mother and grandmother, those summer visits had come to a screeching halt. Kate had vanished from her life, just like the boy from that sweet idyllic summer. Now, here she was, over a decade later, being courted by those same butterflies. It seemed almost fitting that Kate would pop back into her life during the same season as Oren Dunn.

"You mean a lot to her, Susannah. All Kate wants for her one-hundredth birthday is to reconnect with you. I'm honestly starting to think the entire birthday celebration is just a ploy to get you to come." Madeline pulled a face. "Or maybe not. I did, after all, build an entire theme park for this shindig. And did Oliver tell you that there's actual royalty on the guest list?"

Susannah glanced at him on the other side of the yard where he was helping a petite little girl onto the back of a Shetland pony with ribbons braided through its mane. Yet again, she felt an unmistakable tug on her heart. What was going on? She'd been around children plenty of times before without wishing for one of her own.

Hershey snorted, as if to say, *Really? Even I know why you're thinking about marriage and babies all of a sudden.*

Susannah blinked. Marriage hadn't crossed her mind at all…

Until now. She redirected her attention back toward Madeline. What had they been talking about, again? Oh, right. "Royalty? At Kate's party?"

"Yes, there's a branch of the Fortunes who are

royal." Madeline lowered her voice. "Like, with crowns and everything."

A laugh slipped out before Susannah could stop it. "Why am I not surprised?"

The family was already considered Texas royalty. Crowns and real royal titles just made it official.

"I had no idea that Kate wanted to get reacquainted with me so badly," Susannah said, sobering at the idea that her great-great-aunt may have tried to get in touch with her over the years. "My dad would've never gone against my mom's wishes after she passed away. I really have no way of knowing if Kate ever reached out back then."

Would she even have known if Kate had tried to contact her more recently? In Hollywood, Susannah's life had been so carefully managed that entire conversations happened about her, not with her. Her publicist filtered messages, her manager handled her schedule, and her assistant decided which calls and emails reached her at all. It was easier for everyone if she stayed focused on work. And easier still to keep certain things from her entirely.

It was just another example of the downside of fame. The bigger and brighter Susannah's star had shined, the smaller her world had become. It had happened so gradually that she hadn't realized it at first. Then one day, she'd woken up in the hospital and realized the only people coming to see her were paid employees who'd been thoroughly vetted by her security team.

Except for Brett, of course. The bodyguards waved him right through every time. Why wouldn't they? He was her talent manager *and* her fiancé. In the end, he'd hurt her more than any stranger could have.

"I don't mean to pressure you." Madeline offered her a sympathetic smile. "But she's desperate for you to be at the party. She mentions it every single time I talk to her. It almost feels like a dying wish."

Susannah's breath caught in her throat. "You don't mean she's sick, do you?"

"Oh, no." Madeline shook her head and grabbed hold of Susannah's hand, gently squeezing away her panic. "I'm sorry. I didn't mean to frighten you. Kate Fortune is as healthy as a horse and sharp as a tack. She has zero plans for dying anytime soon. I just meant that she's very insistent."

Susannah let out a relieved exhale, although how had Oliver put it, exactly?

She's turning one hundred, Suzy. She might not have many more birthdays left.

If she bailed on this party, there might never be another one.

"I've missed her," Susannah confessed, heart squeezing tight as she thought back on all those Texas summers. "I know my mom and grandmother didn't get along with Kate, but she was always so kind to me, so loving. In her own, no-nonsense way, of course."

"That's Kate, all right." Madeline gave a dry chuckle. "No nonsense."

If she were here right now, she'd probably tell Susannah she needed to get over herself and get on with her life, scars and all. She had to admit it would've been sage advice, especially coming from someone who was about to turn a century old. That kind of perspective was rare.

"Going to that party would be a much bigger step for me than this sweet toddler celebration. I bet the guest list is huge," Susannah said. Dread was already pooling low in her belly just thinking about it.

Madeline rattled off a number, and it barely registered as Susannah's mind whirled with worst-case scenarios. There would be strangers—unlike here, where everyone knew Oliver and treated her kindly. At Forrest's ranch, she was surrounded by friendly faces. But at that party…people would stare. Whisper. Someone might even snap photos for the tabloids.

Susannah threaded trembling fingers through Hershey's soft coat, grounding herself in the familiar comfort of his fur. "If it's okay with you, I'd like to think about it for a little while longer before I commit to being there."

"I get it, Susannah. This isn't a small thing. So yes, absolutely. Take whatever time you need," Madeline said, her voice warm.

"In the meantime, if I get Kate a birthday gift and write something for her in a card explaining that I can't make any promises but I'll do my best to attend, could you arrange for her to get it?" Susannah bit her bottom lip. It wasn't the answer Kate wanted, but it was something. She just hoped it was enough.

Madeline nodded. "I'd be happy to."

Hershey shifted beside Susannah, pressing his weight against her good leg. She let her hand rest just behind his ears, feeling steadier than she had in days.

She might not be ready for a fancy party at the Emerald Ridge Hotel, but she hadn't thought she was ready for today, either.

Maybe she would end up surprising herself, after all.

The baby fever Susannah seemed to be developing *definitely* caught her by surprise.

It wasn't that she'd never thought about having a family. On the contrary, she'd always imagined herself married with children someday. She'd just always thought of being a mother as something she'd do later, once her career slowed down.

Even after she and Brett got engaged, they hadn't really discussed their plans for a family. Susannah had brought it up once or twice, but every time she mentioned it, Brett would remind her that her time in the spotlight was limited. Hollywood was notoriously cruel to women once they started aging. Lead parts didn't go to women in their forties and fifties. She needed to strike while the iron was hot. There would be plenty of time for a personal life later.

Susannah hadn't necessarily agreed, but as her talent manager, Brett always thought of her career first. *He's just doing his job*, she'd told herself. There'd been no reason to worry or feel hurt about his reticence to talk about babies when they hadn't even set a date yet for the wedding.

But now, sitting on a bale of hay while a wide-eyed toddler in denim overalls scampered past her with a giggle, Susannah felt something stir deep inside her. The quiet ache caught her off guard, especially the way it seemed to intensify every time Oliver's eyes met hers. This was more than just baby fever, wasn't it? It was a longing for something she hadn't even realized she'd been missing.

The sound of the children's laughter, the colorful sunset streaking across the sky over the ranch and a big, extended family like the Fortunes—it all painted a picture of a life that was softer…slower…*real*. A life that she'd never had the chance to imagine before, at least not like this. Not with freckled noses, tiny cowboy boots and cupcake frosting tangled in pigtails. Susannah loved her dogs so much, but she wanted this, too…

To be a mother. Heaven help her, she might even want it with Oliver.

"What's that grin for?" he asked as he came to sit down beside her and handed her a bag of corn chips with a fork sticking out of it. Frito pie—warm chili poured straight over corn chips and topped with grated cheddar cheese—was an iconic Texas treat that Susannah hadn't had in years. This party kept getting better and better.

"Nothing in particular." She grinned even harder as she reached to brush a clump of straw from the brim of his Stetson. "I'm just really happy I came today. Thank you for inviting me."

"I'm glad, too." He leaned toward her and gave her a kiss on the cheek. "And there's no need to thank me. Everyone adores you. You now have a standing invitation to all family functions."

"Everyone has been so nice," Susannah said. Hershey's nose twitched as she dug into her Frito pie.

Honey and Bear had planted themselves next to the beanbag toss. Every time a beanbag overshot its mark, one of the Labs retrieved it and dropped it at the player's feet.

"Madeline said you're thinking about attending Kate's one-hundredth birthday party." He looked at her with cautious optimism.

"I told her I needed some time. Maybe." Susannah's stomach tumbled. "We'll see."

Oliver reached for her hand and squeezed it tight. He didn't mention the party again, but she knew if she decided to go, he'd be right there beside her, offering his support.

Everything was happening so fast. She knew she shouldn't be thinking about children when she couldn't even commit to attending a party, let alone rejoining the world in a meaningful way. There was just something about Oliver, though. He made her want things—*dangerous* things, like a normal life, which was awfully hard to imagine after everything they'd both been through in the past year.

Oliver had complicated feelings about his childhood, and Susannah didn't blame him. His mother had refused to tell him who his father was, insisted on changing their names and kept him away from the rest of his family. He hadn't even known that he had an aunt until he'd arrived in Emerald Ridge and found out about Jeralyn Ward. The truth about Archibald was even more of a shock. Did he even want children of his own someday?

She hadn't asked him. It felt too soon and too presumptuous, especially when her own life was still in pieces. He seemed so grounded. But Susannah knew better than most that steadiness could be a performance. She'd spent years perfecting that very act.

Still, the way he looked at her sometimes—like he could see straight into her heart—it made her wonder. Maybe he *did* want that kind of future, even if he couldn't quite picture it yet.

Just like her.

Chapter Nine

Oliver wasn't ready for his time with Susannah to end after he drove her home. Being with her always reminded him of simpler summer days. The party had stretched from early afternoon all the way to evening, but somehow it had passed in a blur. He loved seeing her talk and laugh with his family. It made him think that perhaps she really did want to step back into the world and forge relationships.

But as much as he wanted that for her—connection, healing, joy—he couldn't deny the selfish part of him that didn't want to share her.

The years since they'd spent an entire summer together felt like an eternity and the blink of an eye, both at the same time. Time felt different when he was a kid. The days were long, and the break between school years felt like it stretched on forever. He'd lived an entire lifetime during that summer.

Now that he was a grown man with adult responsibilities, time was his most precious commodity. The ranch, his family, his animals—they all needed his attention, but when he was with Susannah, everything else felt like background noise. Kissing her…touching her…

made him feel like he'd caught summer sunshine in a bottle. He wanted, *needed*, more of that. More of her.

He was falling for Susannah, and he knew his feelings must've been written all over his lovesick face. As they'd said their goodbyes back at Forrest's ranch, Penn's wife, Gia—who was the head of marketing at her family's prestigious winery, Leonetti Vineyards—had handed him a bottle of wine with a knowing smile and told him to enjoy his evening with Susannah.

Now the bottle rested in the center console while Hershey, Honey and Bear dozed in the back, their soft pants filling the quiet car as he clicked off the engine. Neither he nor Susannah said anything at first, and he wondered if she was experiencing the same bittersweet tug now that their date was coming to an end.

And yet, right on the heels of that realization came the unease. He'd already seen how fragile she was beneath her brave front, how much she'd endured. The last thing he wanted was to become one more person who let her down. Trust didn't come easily to him anymore, and the thought of giving his heart only to risk breaking hers made his chest tighten.

She turned to him with a bashful smile playing at the corners of her mouth and said, "Would you like to come inside for a bit?"

His pulse kicked hard, echoing with possibility. "I'd love to."

Together, they got the dogs unloaded and fed. Oliver volunteered to take them outside for a short walk after their dinner, because he could tell the full day had been a lot for Susannah, physically as well as emotionally.

She was moving around a little slower than she normally did and seemed to be relying more on her cane for support. It was a relief when she didn't put up a fight and let him take over dog duty for a few minutes.

Hershey, Honey and Bear seemed confused at first. They lingered in the doorway and kept glancing back at Susannah but eventually followed Oliver's lead. He counted that as a small triumph. He'd always had a way with animals, but those three Labs *lived* for Susannah. She and her dogs were a family. He liked the idea that perhaps Hershey, Honey and Bear were starting to see him as part of their pack.

They didn't stray far and swiveled their heads toward him often as they poked their noses around the wooded area just beyond the deck. Through the log mansion's windows, Oliver could see Susannah moving gingerly around the living room, setting out wineglasses and starting a fire in the tempered glass electric fireplace.

"You were supposed to be resting," he chided when he ushered the dogs back inside.

All three of them trotted straight toward Susannah, tongues lolling. As soon as she showered them with praise, they curled up on their dog beds, chins dropping to their paws like they'd finally run out of steam. Spending the day at Forrest's ranch had apparently taken a toll on them, too.

"I'm fine," Susannah said as she spread a quilt over her lap and crooked a finger for him to come sit beside her. "You don't have to fuss over me. I'm used to doing things on my own."

"Maybe I *like* fussing over you. Ever think of that?" he retorted, settling beside her and reaching for the corkscrew and the bottle of wine in the center of the rustic coffee table. "Besides, just because you're used to going it alone doesn't mean you have to keep doing it."

He poured her a glass of wine and handed it to her, and when she took it without fully meeting his gaze, he wondered if he'd overstepped.

She'd been through a lot the past year—more than he'd ever really understand. Clearly, she didn't like to talk about the accident or her recovery. But he wanted her to know that her scars didn't scare him—not the physical kind, and not the invisible wounds that cut even deeper. He wasn't going to run off and leave her like that other guy had.

"You deserve someone to share your life with, Suzy," he said quietly as she sipped her wine.

He reached for her legs and gently pulled them across his thighs. When her eyes finally locked with his, they were soft and shimmering with unshed tears. She still didn't say anything, but that look alone was enough for him to realize she might finally be ready to show him all her vulnerability. All her fragile hope.

The thought nearly undid him. He only hoped he was worthy of it. Worthy of her trust, her heart, and this quiet, trembling moment between them. Because as much as he wanted to be the one she could lean on, a part of him still worried he'd fall short. He'd never had an example of steady, lasting love to model his own heart after. His parents' tangled mess of lies and broken promises had taught him more about leaving than staying.

"I know you don't need anyone to take care of you, but I sure wish you'd let me," he said, and heaven help him, his voice cracked before he could even get the words out.

"You have no idea how badly I want that…how badly I want us." She took a deep breath and met his gaze without flinching. "What I'm trying to say is that I want *you*, Oliver Fortune."

Longing surged through him as he set down his wineglass, then took hers and placed it on the table so he could lift her closer, so she was fully sitting in his lap within proper kissing distance.

"Yeah?" he asked, gently nipping her bottom lip as his hand curved around the back of her neck. Her loose golden waves were like spun silk against his rough fingertips.

"Oh, yes." She smiled against his lips, and that was all the invitation he needed.

He kissed her, slow and tender, taking his time. There was no rush. The sweet summer days had always belonged to them, and if Oliver had any say in the matter, they always would.

"Oliver," she whispered, and the tremble in her voice wasn't fear or hesitation like it had been back when they'd first run into each other on the day he'd trespassed onto her property. It was yearning. It was desire and reverence, all wrapped up into a delicious ache. Oliver knew that, because that same ache had burrowed under his skin, into his very soul… "You don't need to hold back. I'm not perfect, but I'm also not made of glass."

"Later on, we're going to talk about just how perfect you really are," he growled as he scooped her up and carried her past the fireplace, toward her bedroom.

It was nothing short of a miracle when he realized he didn't hear the pitter-patter of Labrador paws on his heels. The next time he came over, he was going to bring them each a marrowbone the size of a baseball bat from the meat market downtown.

"Later, huh?" She grinned up at him as they crossed the threshold of her room and he kicked the door shut behind him. "Why not now?"

"Because now I've got something better in mind, sweetheart," he said.

She giggled as he tossed her playfully onto the bed, because after all, she'd said herself she wasn't made of glass. Looking at her now, all flushed cheeks and fire in her eyes, he believed her.

And he sure as shooting wasn't going to make her say it twice.

Hours later, Susannah wrapped a blanket around her shoulders as she stepped out onto the deck. It was nearly midnight, but she was too happy to close her eyes and go to sleep, too full of warmth and wonder to let the evening end.

She glanced up at the sky and her heart swelled. The stars shone so brightly out here in the country, unlike her house in the Hollywood Hills, where urban glow drowned out the constellations. She always went a little breathless when she first stepped out on the deck after dark. Deep down, she hoped that feeling would never fade—that all this glittering starlight wouldn't become something taken for granted, like the summers of her childhood.

Susannah hadn't realized how special that time in her life had been until it was gone…until her family stopped coming to Texas and Oliver, the river, those long golden afternoons—all of it—faded into nothing more than a cherished memory. Now she knew how precious it had been, and she didn't want to lose it again. Not this time. Not when a happy-ever-after was finally within reach.

She pulled the blanket more snugly around her just as footsteps echoed on the wooden planks behind her. Oliver stepped onto the deck, and a slow smile spread across his handsome face when he saw her standing there in the moonlight.

"Here you are." He moved closer, reaching out to tuck a stray lock of hair behind her ear. "I woke up and you were gone."

She leaned into his touch until her cheek was cradled in the palm of his hand. An uncontainable smile tugged at the corners of her mouth. "Sorry. I couldn't sleep."

He pressed a kiss to her forehead. "Do you want to tell me why that's a good thing? Because you look as happy as a cat in a sunbeam right now."

"It was a great day. I wanted to hold on to it a little longer." She swallowed, and suddenly, it all felt too good to be true. She hadn't let herself dream of this kind of happiness in such a long time. Now that she'd found joy, it scared her how much she wanted it to last. She didn't even mind that she'd just checked her phone to see if the literary agent had gotten back to her yet and found her inbox empty, as usual. "I just didn't want it to end, that's all. Does that make sense?"

"It makes perfect sense," he said, his voice velvety soft in the darkness. "I didn't want it to end, either. And the best part is—we don't have to let it. How about I get that bottle of Leonetti wine and we can sit out here and enjoy the view for a bit?"

"I'd like that a lot." She wrapped her arms around her middle, if only to keep herself from full-on melting at this man's feet.

As happy as a cat in a sunbeam.

Hershey, Honey and Bear might object to that particular figure of speech since they were dogs, but Susannah had to admit it perfectly described the way she felt. The cool night air nipped at her shoulders as she got situated on the cedar settee and placed her cell phone on the table, but the warmth of Oliver's touch remained, like the fading heat from those old bonfires they'd huddled around as kids.

Oliver returned holding the opened bottle of wine in one hand and two glasses in the other, the elegant stems balanced neatly between his fingers. He poured her a glass and then sat down beside her, pulling her legs into his lap like he'd done earlier. She took a sip and then groaned as he began to expertly massage her feet.

"Just when I thought today couldn't get any better," she said, letting her eyes drift shut as she tipped her head back onto the smooth wood of the arm of the settee.

"I love seeing you like this, Suzy Q," he murmured.

She cracked one eye open. "Relaxed?"

"Happy," he corrected with a lopsided grin. "You can't stop smiling, can you, beautiful girl?"

Susannah's cheeks went warm, but this time she didn't look away. For once, she actually believed him, and not just because of the way he said it. He'd just made love to her like she was precious and rare—like every scar and imperfection was something he cherished, not something he looked past.

"You're right, I can't," she admitted thickly.

"Tell me something." He gave her foot a tender squeeze. "Are you honestly glad you came to the toddler party today?"

"Honestly?"

He nodded. "Yes."

"I loved every minute of it."

"Even the baby goats?" The corner of his mouth quirked up. "Because those little guys were relentless."

Susannah gasped. "They were cute!"

"Except when they were headbutting my shins." He laughed and shook his head.

She swatted him with a throw pillow. "You're fine. Those adorable things didn't stand a chance against your leather Luccheses."

A dimple flashed in his left cheek. "What was your favorite thing about the party? Other than the goats, obviously."

Watching you with the children.

Susannah bit her tongue before the words came flying out of her mouth. It was too soon to say something like that, wasn't it? He'd probably go running for the hills if she admitted she was already fantasizing about having his babies.

Then again, Oliver would know in an instant if she was lying. He'd always been able to see the real her—even when no one else could. She'd been an actress for her entire adult life, but that version of herself felt like a wholly different person. She didn't want to perform anymore, especially with him.

"I liked seeing you with your nieces and nephews." She hesitated and let the rest of the truth tumble out. "You really have a way with children."

Oliver gave her a sideways glance. "You think so?"

"Absolutely. You're going to be a great dad someday." She squirmed a little under his gaze. "Assuming that's something you want. Have you ever thought about it? Starting a family?"

Another crooked grin spread across his face. "Am I detecting a note of baby fever in this line of questioning?"

"Maybe…" Susannah had difficulty swallowing all of a sudden. Why was her heart beating so hard in her chest? And why did she die a little bit inside when his smile seemed to stiffen in place? "Would that be so terrible?"

"Of course it isn't terrible. Your hopes and dreams are important to me. I want you to have everything your heart desires," he said, but the hesitation in his tone resonated much louder than his actual words.

"But?" Susannah prompted. She slid her legs from his lap and sat up straighter so she could reach for her wineglass.

"But I'm not sure I can get there, given my past," he admitted. His voice sounded oddly detached. Wooden, almost. "My mom raised me on her own, and for a long time I thought that was enough. Then I found out who my father really was. He was a man with multiple families, like the rules never applied to him. It kind of messes with your idea of what family's supposed to mean."

This was all her fault. She'd known from the start that it was much too soon to talk about starting a family. She took a gulp of her Leonetti Chardonnay, buying for time.

Still, he'd acted so open around her. He'd invited her to meet his family, for goodness' sake. She didn't need him to tell her that he couldn't wait to have children with her, but the sudden shift in his demeanor was concerning. Maybe Oliver was more closed off emotionally than he'd let on.

"I can understand why you might feel that way," she whispered, doing her best to keep her smile in place. But it wobbled off her face, all the same.

They sat there for a few silent moments, and Susannah almost wished he would go ahead and leave. She needed some time to process everything that had happened today. She'd jumped in with both feet, and now she was wondering if it had been a mistake. Maybe she'd been better off hunkering down in the woods with her dogs.

"Susannah, I—" Oliver started, and whatever he was going to say, she wasn't sure she wanted to hear it.

She didn't blame him for having trust issues, after learning the truth about his parents. But what, exactly, was he so afraid of? Did he think he might get married, have a baby and suddenly turn into Archibald? That's not how bigamy worked. It wasn't contagious. Susannah knew without a doubt that Oliver would never betray someone he loved like that.

"I didn't mean to make you uncomfortable. We really don't have to talk about this," she said.

What she *wanted* to say was that he deserved happiness as much as she did. How was it even possible that he had so much faith in her but so little in himself? Now wasn't the time, though. They'd been on a handful of dates and slept together once. It was much too soon to even have this discussion. She'd gotten carried away, that's all…swept up in the newness of hope after believing her future was so utterly hopeless for such a long time.

Somewhere deep down, Susannah knew it was more than that, though. She wanted to live again. *Really* live. The accident had nearly killed her, and she'd spent the past year licking her wounds. Now that she was beginning to heal, she didn't want to waste any more time. That's why she'd wanted Oliver to take her to bed— not because she'd gotten swept up in the moment, but because now that she knew what she wanted her future to look like, she wanted to take hold of it with both hands and never let go.

It hadn't really occurred to her that the man she'd

fallen for might not be ready. They'd both been through so much. Maybe *too* much…

"Suzy Q," he rasped, and the tenderness in his voice nearly made her eyes fill.

Suddenly, her cell phone rang, and the delicate intimacy of the moment came to an abrupt end. Under any other circumstances, Susannah would've ignored the interruption, but in this case, it gave her a reason to look away and gather herself. A welcome distraction, indeed.

It was awfully late, though. Who could possibly be calling her at this hour?

She glanced at the screen and gasped.

No. She had to be seeing things. *No possible way.*

Oliver shifted beside her, brow furrowing. "Everything okay?"

"Um," she said, and that was all she could manage.

No, everything was most definitely *not* okay. There, lit up in bold white letters, was a name she hadn't seen on her screen in a year.

Brett.

Chapter Ten

Before she fully realized what she was doing, Susannah snatched the phone off the table and answered the call.

She hadn't even meant to do it. She had no desire whatsoever to talk to Brett. *Ever.* But the shock of seeing his name on the display screen had rendered her immobile. Then muscle memory must've kicked in, because by the third ring, she'd tapped the green "accept call" button. Now the phone was pressed to her ear, and there was no taking it back.

"Susannah?" His voice sounded exactly the same— smooth, confident and all too familiar.

Beside her, Oliver mouthed, "Are you okay?"

A lump rose to the back of her throat. Susannah didn't respond to either of them right away. She couldn't. Her hand clenched around the phone so tightly that her knuckles went white.

"I wasn't sure you'd pick up," Brett continued, his tone gentler now, laced with something that might've been regret. Or manipulation. With him, it was hard to tell.

In hindsight, too much of their relationship had been

transactional. Susannah realized that now. She'd been his biggest client, which meant that his finances were inextricably tied up in hers. Every time she made a dime, Brett got a cut. All the attention and flattery he'd heaped on her hadn't meant he loved her at all. She'd simply been his most valuable meal ticket, and once the gravy train was over, there'd been no reason for him to stay.

It was truly a wonder how much clarity could come from healing.

Oliver rested his hand on her thigh, tentative but visibly alarmed. "Susannah?" His eyes darted to the phone, then back to her face, full of concern.

She blinked, drew in a steadying breath and looked away, forcing her voice to stay flat. "What do you want, Brett?"

The man had dumped her when she was at her most vulnerable and made her feel like she was an unlovable beast, so dispensing with the niceties seemed acceptable. If she hadn't been so rattled, she would've simply hung up.

"I'm sorry, Susannah. I've done a lot of maturing over this past year, and I realize now that I treated you terribly." Brett cleared his throat. "I want you to know how deeply sorry I am about everything—the accident itself, obviously, but mostly about that last conversation we had at the hospital. If I could take back all the terrible things I said that day, I would do it in a heartbeat."

Susannah wasn't sure what she'd expected, but it definitely hadn't been an apology. In all the years she'd known Brett, she'd never heard him say he was sorry.

For *anything*. That alone should've been a red flag. She'd always chalked it up to his profession, though. For agents and talent managers in show business, it was a kind of power play. She hadn't realized his inability to utter the words *I'm sorry* carried over to his personal life until after the engagement ring was already on her finger.

"Why are you telling me this now, Brett?" she asked, and much to her mortification, there was a crack in her voice.

She didn't want his apology to matter. This man was her past, and he had no part whatsoever in her future. It was still good to hear him admit how wrong he'd been, though. Vindication, at long last.

"Like I said, I was wrong about a lot of things. I know better than to think that you and I have any kind of future together, romantically speaking. But, babe, I think you could have a whole new film career, even bigger and brighter than before." He paused, seemingly for dramatic effect, and Susannah almost threw up in her mouth when she heard him call her *babe*. Gross. "Scratch that—I don't just think so, I know so. I've already talked to a few studio heads, and we've got actual offers on the table."

"B-but…" Susannah stammered. What good were new film offers when no one in Hollywood knew about her disfigurement? The second they saw her new face, the studio executives would change their minds.

"Before you object, they already know everything. They don't care. In fact, they think it would make you more relatable. Come on, Susannah, you know how much everyone loves an underdog story." Brett softened his tone, his voice gentler now. "I don't mean that in a bad way. You'll always be a star, no matter what. No one can take that away from you."

"I don't know, Brett. This is all very sudden and completely out of the blue." She didn't even want to star in movies anymore. She'd put that dream to bed.

Hadn't she?

She glanced at Oliver, and his eyes searched her face, worry etched on his expression. She could feel the tension radiating off him, like he was bracing for whatever this conversation might bring.

Nothing, she told herself. *This call doesn't have to change anything.*

"I think we should meet," Brett said, and she shifted her gaze to her lap. Talking to her ex didn't feel right while Oliver sat silently beside her, clearly unsettled.

Not that she'd done anything wrong…and not that she and Oliver were even on the same page about the future. That had become painfully clear just a few minutes ago.

"Let me come down to Emerald Ridge," Brett continued. "We can go over the details of your comeback in person. I can be there as early as tomorrow."

"No," Susannah blurted.

There was a pause on the other end of the line.

"I just… I need to think," she added, her voice steadier now. "I'll call you if I decide anything."

She didn't wait for Brett's reply. Her thumb hovered for half a second, then she ended the call and set the phone face down on the table like it might burn her if she didn't rid herself of it as soon as humanly possible.

The stillness of the night pressed in around her. What had felt calm and peaceful moments ago now seemed stifling.

She wasn't sure what to say to Oliver. Every time she tried to speak, the words clogged in her throat. This was all so awkward. She glanced over at him, wishing he would be the first to break the silence.

Oliver didn't utter a word, though. He didn't have to.

The hurt in his eyes said enough.

The moonlight bathed Susannah's face in silver, making her look almost ghostlike. Too motionless, too pale. Oliver hated how distant she suddenly seemed, like she was halfway back into the life she'd left behind in California. He didn't know the extent of the conversation she'd just had, but he knew enough to recognize the hollow ache in her eyes. Enough to wonder what, exactly, this loser thought he was doing, calling her like that.

"That wasn't what you think," Susannah said, finally tearing her gaze away from the phone to look at him. She'd been staring at the device like she was in a trance for nearly a full minute since she'd plunked it face down on the table.

"So that wasn't Brett, your ex-fiancé?" he asked, knowing full well that he'd been the caller.

Oliver knew he didn't have any real claim on Susannah. Hadn't he just finished telling her he wasn't sure he'd ever feel ready to start a family? It wouldn't be fair to expect her to wait around for him to get himself together if she was truly ready for babies and children.

They'd just found each other again, however. With all the turmoil they'd both been through recently, he knew the timing wasn't perfect—far from it. But having her back in his life after all those years felt like more than coincidence. It felt like…a long-awaited happy ending he didn't even know he'd been hoping for.

"Yes, that was Brett." She gnawed on her bottom lip and averted her gaze. "But it wasn't personal. It was business-related."

Again, she didn't owe him an explanation. But today had been special. Something had shifted between them, and this evening, they'd shared a bed.

Making love to her, holding her close afterward and feeling her heartbeat steady against his had felt like coming home to a place he hadn't realized he'd been missing his whole life. For a few fleeting hours, all the noise in his head had gone quiet. She'd trusted him, let him in, and he'd let himself believe, just for a moment, that maybe he could trust her, too.

Now, that fragile peace was slipping away, and Oliver's stomach was tying itself into an ugly, jealous knot.

Was her ex hoping to get back together with Susannah after the awful way he'd treated her? Oliver certainly hoped not, and not just because he had feelings for her himself. She deserved better than the likes of Brett. Couldn't she see that? He knew she'd come a long way lately. But had she healed enough to fully realize just how incredible she was?

"Sweetheart," he said, gut churning. "I know there's probably a lot I don't know, but from everything you've told me about Brett, he seems untrustworthy, at best. I'd hate to see you get hurt again."

Susannah's eyes narrowed. "I told you it's not like that. Even if it were, I would never take him back again. I have no feelings whatsoever for him."

But she has them for you, and you all but told her you wouldn't want her to have your baby.

He'd wanted to explain. He'd *tried* to, but she'd cut him off, eager to change the subject. And then that jerk had called, and now it was too late.

Was it possible the interruption had been a blessing in disguise? Even if his reasons for reaching out were purely professional, Brett represented the life Susannah had lost—a life she *claimed* she no longer wanted. She hadn't told her ex that, though. Whatever he'd proposed, she hadn't immediately shot down, like Oliver would've expected. She'd said she needed *to think.*

If this was her new life—the life she wanted to fill with mystery books, rescue dogs and babies—what was there to think about?

Maybe Susannah wanted her old life back more than she'd realized.

"I hear what you're saying. I just—" Oliver's teeth clenched. He really needed to choose his words carefully before he said something he might regret.

"You just don't believe me." The look she gave him was a knife to the heart. "Got it."

This entire night had gone completely off the rails, and Oliver would've loved nothing more than to set the blame for it squarely at Brett's feet. But he knew it was partially his fault. The second Susannah wanted more from him than he was ready to give, he'd shut down emotionally. She'd noticed right away. *Of course* she had. She knew him better than anyone else, even his newfound siblings.

He'd been naive and trusting when they'd met. Now, not so much. How was he supposed to form meaningful and authentic connections with the rest of the Fortunes when he constantly kept his guard up, waiting for the inevitable moment when one of them let him down? Like Archibald…like his mother…

"That's not it at all. It's not that I don't trust you," Oliver said. Wasn't it, though? He was trying his absolute best not to close himself off, but it wasn't so much a choice as an automatic reaction, like the fight-or-flight response. It was a survival mechanism—his mind and body's way of making sure he never got blindsided by someone he loved again.

Love. His heart hammered against his rib cage. *Is that what this is?*

If he was really in love, wouldn't he find it easier to promise Susannah he could give her whatever she wanted…and needed? Would he ever be able to let go like that again?

"Brett thinks I could make a big career comeback in Hollywood," she told him quietly. "If that's what I want."

Oliver felt himself frown. "Is it?"

She hadn't mentioned wanting to go back to show

business at all—not even once. He hadn't even realized a comeback was on the table.

Susannah hadn't either, apparently.

"No, it's not," she said, but her response came too quickly. It sounded like a knee-jerk reaction instead of a thoughtful answer. "I think I'm just confused. That call caught me off guard."

Yeah, him, too.

"I think I'm going to get going," he said gruffly. He stood before he changed his mind, since leaving was the last thing he really wanted to do.

If he stayed, though, he'd just get even more tangled up in whatever was developing between them. Tonight had been a literal wake-up call. He needed time to think. So did she, whether she wanted to admit it to him or not.

"You don't have to go, Oliver." She looked up at him, and the anguish in her eyes made them look greener than ever in the moonlight. They glittered like fine emeralds.

He forced down his rising emotions, jaw clenched, and muttered something about having an early morning tomorrow.

It was just an excuse, and they both knew it. Oliver wasn't fooling anyone—not even her dogs. Because the last thing he heard after he'd gotten dressed, gathered his Stetson and walked out the front door was the hushed, mournful sound of Hershey, Honey and Bear whining behind him.

Chapter Eleven

Oliver kept as busy as he possibly could for the next few days. Now that Forrest and Nick were helping out with the design of the new ranch, things were moving full steam ahead. There was enough work to keep himself occupied from sunup to sundown, and that's precisely what he chose to do.

The day after Brett's phone call, Susannah had texted him a picture she'd snapped of her dogs running ahead of her on her morning walk, tails wagging as the sun spilled gold over the dewy grass. Unlike all her previous messages, she hadn't included any words, only the image. Oliver hadn't known what to say, so he'd "liked" it and that was that. Since then, their constant stream of messages and phone calls had come to a screeching halt.

He kept thinking that once Susannah had enough time to consider a comeback, she'd realize it wasn't what she truly wanted. Then she'd tell Brett to go take a hike—and call him. But as the silence between them stretched from one day to the next, the doubts he'd been trying to keep away pushed in from every side.

Now, here he was, midweek—Wednesday, to be

exact—without a clue as to where they stood. The space he'd thought he'd needed felt like a great, yawning chasm. Oliver wasn't sure he knew how to get back to the other side.

He ground his teeth as he strode into Donatello's Pizzeria on his way back to the hotel from the ranch. As usual, the front area for walk-in slices and to-go orders was packed. Everyone in Emerald Ridge loved Donatello's. Oliver hoped he could dash inside, pick up his large pepperoni order and dash back out without running into anyone he knew. He wasn't in the mood for chitchat. He wanted pizza. Period.

But, of course, the second he stepped inside, he nearly collided with another Fortune.

"Oliver!" Madeline's face brightened as she shifted the stack of flat cardboard boxes and take-out bags in her hands. "It's so great to bump into you."

He touched the brim of his Stetson with a nod at his sister. "Good to see you, too."

"I'd hug you but my hands are kind of full." She laughed and glanced down at the handful of pizza boxes and Donatello's sacks she was juggling.

"No worries at all. Let me give you a hand with those." He was stuck now, so he might as well make himself useful. He grabbed the pizza boxes and held the door open for her with one of his boots. "Where are you parked?"

"Just down the street." She nodded toward her luxury vehicle, instantly recognizable with the Let's Get This Party Started logo emblazoned on the driver's side door.

Oliver headed in the right direction. "I'll help you load up. I'm assuming all this is for one of your parties?"

"Sort of, but not technically." Her stilettos click-clacked on the pavement as she walked. "I'm having one last planning meeting to go over the details for Kate Fortune's one-hundredth birthday party. There's a lot to go over, so I figured I should feed my crew."

"That's nice of you," Oliver said, longing for a way to change the subject before his sister asked him if Susannah had decided whether she would attend.

"The party is *this* Saturday. You know that, right?" Madeline aimed an expectant glance his way.

"Mads, this party has taken on epic proportions. Do you seriously think I'm going to forget?" He wished he could—because the truth was, he was running out of time to figure things out with Susannah before the celebration. Oliver certainly didn't want to be the reason she decided not to attend.

"I'm just making sure it's on your radar. Forrest said you haven't really been yourself lately." Madeline stopped next to her vehicle, piling her take-out bags on top of the pizza boxes in Oliver's arms, then fishing around in her huge designer handbag for her car keys.

"I'm fine. Just been busy." Oliver loaded the food into her car and waited for her to climb behind the wheel and drive off, but she didn't seem in any big hurry to leave.

She looked him up and down as she twirled the keys around her finger. Her engagement ring sparkled in the soft evening light. "If you say so. But you promise you're going to be there, right? All of our brothers and sisters are going to attend, plus the moms."

Oliver nodded. There was no getting out of it, no matter how miserable he felt. "You have my word."

"Great." Madeline beamed at him. She'd worked so hard on this party. He really needed to at least pretend to be somewhat excited about it. "At least you won't have to come far. We've got activities planned all afternoon at the mini-amusement park—especially for the kids. But the main party will be on the grounds of the Emerald Ridge Hotel, spilling from the huge grand ballroom onto a large outdoor balcony. All of that starts at 5 p.m. sharp."

He squinted. "And lasts until…?"

"Until Kate is ready to call it a night," his sister said with a laugh. "You might want to prepare yourself for a late night. She's about to turn one hundred, but she can be a bit of a spitfire. I wouldn't dare try and tell her what time her party should end."

He chuckled. "Sounds like an interesting lady."

"You don't know the half of it. I'm excited for you to meet her. She tires easily nowadays, but she also *bores* easily. I have no way of knowing if she'll want to discuss our family drama or answer any questions about Archibald. I doubt she'd be upset if we asked about it, though. Kate is always proper and respectful—she'd never be outright rude to anybody." Madeline tucked a loose lock of hair back into her coppery updo and flashed him a knowing grin. "Unless they deserve it."

The corners of Oliver's mouth tugged into a grin. "Duly noted."

Then, just as he was beginning to relax, she asked the question he'd been dreading. "Has Susannah made up her mind about whether or not she's coming? I sure hope so!"

"I…um…" He let his voice drift off without giving a direct answer. Then he squinted again at the setting sun and shrugged. "I haven't seen Susannah in a few days. Like I said, I've been busy."

"Busy," she echoed, regarding him through narrowed eyes. "Are you sure you're okay? If you need to talk about anything, I'm here. I know you're used to going it alone since you grew up as an only child, just like I did. But I hear that's what big sisters are for."

Oliver crossed his arms. "I'm a year older than you are, Mads."

"I know that, silly." The smile she gave him was full of warmth and genuine concern. "But I feel protective of you. I can't help it. I can't imagine what it must have been like for you when your mom got sick. I wish we'd known about each other back then."

Oliver sure as heck didn't want to talk about his mother right now. But maybe it wouldn't be so bad to open up about Susannah…just a little bit?

He didn't say anything at first, thinking maybe Madeline would take the hint and head out, what with a car full of pizza getting colder by the second. She didn't budge, though. She just stood there like she had all the time in the world to help him with his problems.

"I'm not really used to talking about my feelings," he finally admitted. "I could probably use some practice in that department."

"No time like the present," she said gently, her voice a calm nudge rather than a push.

Oliver sighed. "I guess I might not be all that fine."

Madeline tilted her head, and her expression was so kind that it chipped away at the wall he'd been so busy building around his heart, brick by brick. "This is about Susannah, isn't it?"

Darn. Was he *that* obvious?

"Yes," he admitted, and it felt like something heavy settled behind his sternum. He cleared his throat and continued, "Let's just say that I thought she felt one way about her future…about *me*…and now I'm not so sure."

"Susannah cares about you, Oliver. All of us can see it." The corner of Madeline's mouth quirked up. "You should've seen the way she was watching you interact with the kids at the toddler party."

The pressure in his chest multiplied tenfold and he looked away.

Perhaps the sudden distance between them was a good thing. She wanted children, and he still didn't know if he'd ever be ready after the way he'd grown up. Whether she returned to show business or not, their relationship could only end in disaster.

"Can I give you some sisterly advice?" Madeline asked, shielding her eyes from the amber light of sunset.

He nodded, and he had to admit that being part of a big family like the Fortunes wasn't the worst thing in the world. He might even get used to it someday.

"Talk to Susannah. Ask her what she's thinking instead of trying to figure it out all on your own. You're a great rancher, Oliver, but unraveling the mystery of what women are thinking takes some serious detective skills." She winked at him. "No offense, but you're not Nancy Drew."

His heart gave a little tug at the mention of Susannah's favorite book character. Could it be a sign? Maybe he should heed his sister's advice and reach out. Trying to forget Susannah sure wasn't working. No matter what she decided about her future, he wasn't going to stop caring about her.

He'd tried to guard his heart, but somewhere along the way, falling for Susannah hadn't become a choice. Now it just felt like breathing. Automatic…constant…

And impossible to quit.

Susannah tried her best to put the conversation with Brett completely out of her head. Unfortunately, as the days marched on without any sort of meaningful interaction with Oliver, mulling over the possibility of a Hollywood comeback was the only thing that kept her from thinking about him.

Every time his handsome, chiseled face popped into her mind, she redirected her attention to her acting career—or lack thereof. She thought she'd made peace with ending that chapter of her life. But maybe she'd been fooling herself. If the accident had never happened, would she have willingly left Tinseltown behind and moved to Texas?

Susannah knew the answer was no. Being a famous actress had never been her dream, but once it became her life, she wasn't sure how to step away, or if she even should. The fame, the attention, the sense of purpose it gave her…they'd become a kind of armor she didn't know how to live without. If Brett's car had never crashed through that guardrail, she'd still be making movies, and she'd still be wearing the flashy, ostentatious diamond ring that Brett had given her on her most important finger.

Would the wedding invitations have gone out, though? Would she be dreaming of babies and children and a house in the country with a wraparound porch and a trio of Labrador retrievers in the yard?

Sadly, the answer to those questions was also no. What she and Brett once had together had never been real. Susannah thought it was at the time, but now she knew better. Now, it was all crystal clear.

Here in Emerald Ridge, she'd gotten a glimpse of what real love looked like. Not the dazzling, whirlwind kind that left you feeling breathless and topsy-turvy, but the steady, soul-deep sort that made you understand how to feel comfortable in your own skin. The kind of love that grew from quiet conversations, shared silences and the solid presence of someone who saw you—really and truly *saw* you—and stayed anyway.

Susannah had found that kind of love with Oliver. Or at least she thought she had…

She knew she was expecting too much from him. Baby fever wasn't a contagious condition, after all. Still, it would've been really nice if he'd given her some sort of reassurance that she wasn't alone in her feelings. *I care deeply about you. I just need some time* would've done the trick.

An *I love you* would've been even better.

She'd been so relieved when her phone rang in the middle of that awkward conversation. Talk about being saved by the bell! Never in a million years, though, would she have guessed who'd been calling. Now, four days later, she wasn't the least bit surprised to see her ex's name pop up on her display screen—*again.*

"I thought I told you I needed time to think," she said in lieu of a greeting. Honestly, the guy was relentless. He'd called every single day since that initial phone call, and each and every time, she'd let it roll to voicemail. Now, she just needed it to stop.

Brett's aggressive persistence was probably one of the qualities that made him a good talent manager. As a human being, not so much. Once upon a time, he'd pursued her romantically with the same sort of zeal. Back then, she'd mistaken his relentless efforts for affection. She'd fallen for it, hook, line and sinker. After they'd been dating for a while, she recognized his actions as part of his usual playbook—the way he courted clients, closed deals and bulldozed his way through any obstacle that stood between him and what he wanted. She just hadn't realized *she'd* been one of those obstacles.

Looking back, Susannah could see it so clearly. The grand gestures, the extravagant gifts, the way he always seemed to say the exact right thing…none of it had been about her. It had been about winning.

"I'm sorry, babe," Brett said without sounding the least bit contrite. "Of course you need time to think, but you still don't have all the facts. As your manager, I think it's best for you to understand what exactly they're offering before you make your decision."

He had a point, she supposed.

Hershey dropped a stick at her feet, and Susannah picked it up and threw it for him to fetch. The other dogs chased after him while she stood rooted to the spot on the trail just beyond her back deck with the phone pressed to her ear. It was Wednesday evening during the golden hour, that special sliver of time when the sunset painted the sky in brilliant streaks of gold and amber. Brett, her career and California all seemed very far away.

"Fine. Give me the details," she said with a resigned sigh. Might as well get this part over with so she could give him a definitive no and they could both get on with their lives.

"I was hoping you'd say that." There was a hint of triumph in Brett's voice—subtle, but very much there. "That's why I got on the plane."

"Plane?" She glanced up at the sky as if she expected to see him parachuting toward her with a studio contract and a pen in his hand. Which, now that she thought about it, wouldn't have been all that surprising. "What are you talking about?"

"I caught the red-eye from LA to Dallas late last night, got a rental car at the airport and drove the rest of the way. I'm here in Emerald Ridge so I can apologize to you in person. I really am sorry, Susannah. About everything..."

Her throat went thick, despite herself. Hershey returned with his stick, and this time, when he dropped it at her feet, she barely noticed.

Brett was *here*. In Texas.

"I— Wow. I really don't know what to say." She wrapped her arms around herself. Surely he didn't think she was going to invite him to her home. He was the last person she wanted to invade her little slice of Lone Star paradise.

"Say you'll meet with me so we can discuss what's on offer. All I'm asking is for an hour of your time. Two tops." When she didn't answer right away, he added in a cajoling tone, "*Strictly business*. I'll even book the conference room here at my hotel if you'd prefer that over going to dinner. How's first thing tomorrow morning?"

Susannah exhaled a mildly relieved breath. She hated the thought of going out in public, but not as much as she loathed the idea of Brett anywhere near her log mansion. It was bad enough that he'd already wormed his way into her town.

Maybe she should go ahead and hear him out. What if the offer was for her dream project? She'd always wanted to take on one of Grace Kelly's iconic roles, like her character in *Rear Window* or *Dial M for Murder*. Unlikely, given her change in appearance. No one called Susannah Simmons the next Grace Kelly anymore.

Still, the comeback plan had to be good if Brett had flown all the way here to pitch it face-to-face. And it wasn't like her career as a mystery novelist was going anywhere. The literary agent still hadn't gotten back to her about her manuscript. She hadn't even received a return message to her initial email. Every time she checked her inbox and found it empty, her dreams of becoming a published author seemed further out of reach.

She knew she should just keep writing and improving her craft, and she would. Dreams didn't come true overnight. But the longer she went without hearing anything, the louder the tiny voice in the back of her head became. *You're really going to throw away a lucrative career in the hopes you can reinvent yourself? If writing really means that much to you, you could always go back to acting and work on your manuscript in your spare time.*

Would she, though? Most authors had day jobs, but those jobs typically didn't take over their entire lives. Susannah Simmons the movie star wasn't just an actress. She was a whole public persona…a brand.

"Tomorrow morning works," she heard herself say, even as her stomach turned.

"Excellent." He sounded far too pleased with himself, like her agreement to attend a meeting meant a sure victory.

"But just so we're clear, after the meeting, you're leaving. No surprise visits. No lingering around town. No sudden interest in the local real estate market," she said, and her voice didn't quaver.

There was a pause on the other end, and then Brett let out a soft chuckle. "You have my word. I'll be on the next flight out, no matter what you decide."

"Good."

"But I know you'll say yes," he added, his tone turning smooth again, smug in that way she remembered all too well. "You've always had a great head for business, Susannah. I have no doubt you'll make the right choice."

She ended the call without bothering to say goodbye. Then she went back to playing fetch with her dogs in the lavender twilight, wishing she had just a little bit of Brett's confidence. Just when she'd started believing in herself again, everything had suddenly gone sideways.

The right choice?

Susannah wasn't sure she'd recognize it anymore.

Chapter Twelve

Oliver went back inside Donatello's Pizzeria after his chat with Madeline and placed his order, but his mind was in such a whirl that he couldn't remember what he'd asked for. When the hostess handed him a box with his name scrawled on the side of it, the warm scent of pepperoni drifted up. Apparently, he'd been more present than he'd realized.

Present enough to drive straight over to Susannah's ranch and tell her how you feel?

The thought had definitely occurred to him. Talking to Madeline had given him some much-needed clarity. He was in love with Susannah…

And he needed to tell her before it was too late.

If Susannah felt the same, they could figure out the rest later. *Together.* Whether she wanted to go back to Hollywood or stay in Texas, they could deal with it. If Oliver couldn't trust Susannah, he was hopeless. She was *it* for him. He'd known as much since he was fourteen years old.

Finding out the truth about his family had shaken him to his core, but he was trying to get past it. Forming lasting relationships with his new siblings was helping. He'd felt alone for so long. He didn't want to feel that way forever, though. Not if he could help it.

The Emerald Ridge Hotel was abuzz with activity as Oliver carried his pizza through the shiny revolving door. He strode with purpose, a man on a mission. He couldn't wait to talk to Susannah, but he wanted to do it in person. The conversation was too important for texting or talking on the phone. He'd been out at his ranch all day and was in dire need of a shower and sustenance before he showed up at her door with another bouquet of daisies.

Even with his thoughts centered squarely on Susannah, Oliver couldn't help but notice the pair of women behind the front desk dressed in crisp Emerald Ridge Hotel blazers, whispering behind manicured hands.

"I heard she's coming to see one of the guests," one of them said, clutching her phone like she might snap a photo at any moment. "Can you believe it? Susannah Simmons, right here at the Emerald Ridge!"

"It's got to be a romantic rendezvous," the other replied with a knowing smirk. "The manager informed us the guest wants the whole room covered in floral arrangements—fancy roses that Emerald Ridge Floral is flying in from California."

Oliver froze mid-stride, the pizza box suddenly feeling heavier in his hands. His pulse stumbled. There had to be some kind of mistake. Or maybe it was just a rumor. Surely Brett wasn't here in Texas. He couldn't possibly be the mystery guest they were talking about.

"I'm telling you, it's true. She's coming here tomorrow," whispered a third voice, this one coming from the bellhop standing at the helm of a glossy gold luggage cart. He leaned toward the girls at the front desk. "I saw her name on the VIP list dated tomorrow. The guy is already here. I think it's that slick Hollywood agent she was going to marry before she had that horrible accident last year."

The two women gasped, their excitement practically vibrating across the marble floor.

"Oh my gosh!" the first one squealed. "Can you imagine? After everything that happened with that fiancé of hers, maybe they're giving it another shot. Some kind of hush-hush reconciliation?"

"I thought he dumped her," the other said, her voice low and scandal-tinged. "Wasn't he the one driving the car before it crashed? He could've killed her. Either way, he's a total scumbag."

"Doesn't matter." The bellhop shrugged. "The guy upstairs has money—like *Hollywood* money. And taste, apparently. You should see the champagne order he's got on deck for tomorrow. *Cristal.* And chocolate truffles the size of tennis balls."

Oliver's stomach dropped. The scent of pepperoni and melted cheese turned sour in his nose.

He stood there in the middle of the lobby, shoes rooted to the glossy tile, dazed by the blow of it all. Roses. Champagne. A VIP suite. And Susannah.

The guest was obviously Brett. He'd just called Susannah a few days ago, and now he'd flown into town to woo her back. She'd insisted the call had been all business, but clearly that wasn't true.

And if she was coming to meet him…

Oliver's throat tightened. Susannah *never* left her property. It had been a big deal for her to come as his date to a simple family get-together for kids, and that had been much less high-profile than showing up at the fanciest hotel in town. She was still dragging her feet about attending Kate Fortune's one-hundredth birthday party this Saturday, but she apparently had no qualms when it came to reuniting with Brett.

He wasn't stupid. Oliver knew what all of this meant. He just didn't want to believe it as he stood there, invisible in plain sight while the murmurs around him swelled into a blur of betrayal. He knew he shouldn't have let down his guard. He'd loved his mother with his whole heart, and even she'd kept secrets from him…as had his father, and pretty much everyone Oliver had ever cared about.

Why would Susannah be any different?

"He paid for the penthouse suite up front," the concierge said in a hushed voice as he joined the cluster of employees at the front desk. "And he made a special request for privacy, too. No housekeeping, no interruptions of any kind. He said he and Miss Simmons had a lot to talk about."

"Talk?" The bellhop smirked.

One of the women nodded and crossed her arms. "Seriously. Who flies in roses, champagne and special chocolates for a *chat*?"

"You didn't hear it from me, but he booked a private room at Captain's for dinner—the wine cellar room. Total seclusion, no cameras," the concierge whispered.

"That's where the celebrities go when they don't want to be seen."

Oliver felt like the floor might split open underneath him. He'd heard enough. He marched toward the elevator with his dumb pizza, cardboard bending beneath his fingers as he thought about the plan he'd just been concocting to try and win Susannah back.

It was almost laughable—the earnestness, the daisies, all the things he'd been about to say. He'd convinced himself they still had a shot, and all the while, she'd already chosen someone else.

She was coming here…to *Brett*…after all the terrible things he'd said and done. Oliver still didn't know all the details of the accident, but he knew her manager had been behind the wheel. He'd been responsible for Susannah's injuries, and afterward, he hurt her even more by making her believe she was damaged and unlovable.

Unbelievable. His head pounded as he jabbed at the elevator button. *I was nothing but a placeholder until her fiancé came back.*

He should've known to trust his instincts. People lied. *Everyone* lied, apparently. When she'd told him she wanted a whole new life, it was only because she thought her old one had slipped through her fingers. What had happened to starting over? Was she giving up on her dreams of becoming a mystery novelist, just like she was giving up on him?

Worse yet, was she going to have children with Brett now that Oliver had balked when she'd mentioned wanting a baby? She may or may not have lied to him, but he couldn't shake the feeling that this entire episode was at least partially his fault.

He stepped into the elevator. The doors swished closed, replacing the buzz of excited gossip in the lobby with the soft hum of strings playing over the elevator speakers. Oliver vaguely recognized the song as something romantic. Oh, the irony.

He leaned against the back wall and closed his eyes as the elevator began to move, carrying him closer to Brett and the penthouse suite. The fact that their grand romantic reunion was going to take place just a few floors above Oliver's head was the icing on the cake. He had a good mind to go up there and tell the jerk exactly what he thought of him.

He wouldn't, though. Susannah had made her choice, and if stardom and Brett were truly what she desired, he wouldn't stand in her way. After everything, he still wanted her to be happy. Even if it broke him in the process.

He'd been wrong about so much—about what she wanted, about what they meant to each other, about the life he'd only started to let himself believe in. And now he'd never have that bright, glittering future with the girl he'd been in love with for half his life.

But Susannah Simmons would always have a place in his heart.

Whether she ever wanted it or not.

The following morning, Susannah was up before her dogs for a change. Hershey, Honey and Bear stared at her in confusion for a beat, unconvinced that it was really time for their morning walk. It wasn't until she'd slid her feet into her cowboy boots and grabbed her walking stick that they finally rose from their dog beds and trotted to the back door.

While Susannah led them along the meandering trail just beyond the deck, she ran over her plan for the meeting with Brett. One thing was certain: She wanted to look like a million bucks. The last time she'd been face-to-face with Brett, he'd told her she was unrecognizable. What he'd really meant was that she was no longer beautiful, and now she was determined to prove him wrong. She wanted him to eat those words until he choked on them.

She could do it. Susannah had all the necessary tools at her disposal, thanks to an overzealous personal assistant who'd shipped relics from her Hollywood life to Texas after the closing on the log mansion. It would take some work—hence the early wake-up time—but with some concentrated effort, she could make herself look like Susannah Simmons the movie star again. Who knew how many collective hours she'd spent in front of a mirror while her stylist curled her hair for press events and public appearances. Susannah could probably re-create her signature bombshell hairstyle with her eyes closed. Magazines called it "the peekaboo" and compared it to the way Veronica Lake wore her hair back in the 1940s with long, cascading waves in a side part so deep that the hair fell like a curtain over just one eye. It had been Susannah's trademark on red carpets and movie posters, and it never failed to invoke whispers of Old Hollywood. Of glamour and glitz.

The assistant had shipped an entire box of stage makeup, too. Susannah had used it a few times when she'd gone into town. The pancake foundation was thick and opaque enough to cover her scar, but she'd need to apply it in careful layers so it didn't look like a mask.

Somewhere in the back of her closet sat an unpacked box of her old designer clothes, too. She'd come to love the comfortable Western wear she'd been living in since moving to Texas. Susannah just needed her old familiar armor before she even thought about returning to acting or facing the man who'd left her because she was no longer beautiful.

Her throat burned as she turned around and headed back toward the house with the dogs sniffing at her heels. Had those really been Brett's exact words? Yes, they certainly had.

You're not the same beautiful woman I fell in love with.

Remembering them still brought tears to her eyes. She'd tried so hard to forget, to bury the sting of those words beneath her writing, the quiet nights and the steady comfort of her dogs. But some things were just impossible to forget, especially when the pain still lived right beneath the surface, waiting for moments like this to rise and remind her of everything she'd lost.

But Brett was back now, and he was promising her she could reclaim her old life. Her name could be in lights again. All she had to do was say yes.

Anyone would be tempted, Susannah told herself as

she sat down at her vanity and meticulously began applying her makeup.

Behind her, the dogs shifted warily. Honey's ears were flattened to the sides of her head, while Bear dug at the center of his dog bed, refusing to lie down. Even Hershey, the most even-tempered and unbothered of the three, sat watching her with quiet concern and a deep crease in his furry brow.

They knew. Of course they did.

Dogs were intuitive like that, especially a breed as emotionally intelligent as Labrador retrievers. There was a reason that Labs were so often chosen to be trained as service dogs or therapy animals. They were great at picking up on the emotions that humans tried to hide.

"Don't worry about me, guys. It's going to be fine." She sat her makeup applicator sponge on the counter so she could scratch Hershey behind his ears. The chocolate Lab looked up at her with soulful eyes, and for reasons she didn't fully understand, her throat closed up tight.

This was *her* choice, nobody else's. She had no reason to feel guilty about a simple meeting with Brett. Oliver had already made his feelings clear. First, he'd completely frozen when she'd brought up babies. Then, after Brett phoned her, he'd ceased all communication, even though she'd made it clear the call had been strictly about business. Even if it hadn't, though, Oliver didn't trust her. That was the bottom line, wasn't it? He didn't have enough faith in her to picture a real future together. All this time, he'd been waiting for her to let him down, just like everyone else had. She'd seen it in his eyes the moment she'd hung up the phone with Brett. He hadn't even looked all that surprised—more resigned than anything, as if he'd been bracing for the inevitable all along.

Don't cry. You'll mess up your eyeliner. She bit down hard on her bottom lip to stop the flow of tears, and Hershey let out a quiet whine. Then she took a deep breath and refocused her attention on the mirror and putting herself together until she looked like her old self again.

The hotel valet bustled toward her car as soon as she pulled up under the portico. He glanced at the empty passenger seat as if he expected her to be accompanied by a bodyguard or entourage and then he redirected his attention back at her with a beaming smile.

"Good morning, Miss Simmons. Welcome to the Emerald Ridge Hotel," he said after she rolled her window down. She searched his gaze for any hint that he'd noticed the gash on her face, but the makeup had obviously done the trick. "We've been expecting you. The staff has been busy enthusiastically preparing for your arrival."

Seriously? She was here for a simple business meeting. She wasn't even checking in as a guest.

But, of course, Brett had to turn it into a full-blown production. She really should've known better. It was easy to forget how he—and everything that came with life in the spotlight—could make her feel like an animal in a zoo.

"Wonderful. Thank you very much." Her hands shook as she maintained her death grip on the steering wheel.

She hadn't even gotten out of the car yet, and already, she was getting the detached feeling that always came over her when she was about to put on a performance. In the past, she'd thought of it as confidence. That's not what it felt like now, though. It felt...*fake.*

The valet reached for the car door, and she stopped him before he could open it. "Sorry, but I need a minute. Is that okay?"

He blinked. "Um, sure. Can I get you some water or anything?"

Water wasn't going to help this disaster-in-the-making. Nothing was.

"No, thank you." She pointed to an area up ahead and to the left of the hotel entrance. "I'm just going to pull over there for a quick second."

"Yes, ma'am." The valet nodded. "Just let me know if you need anything—anything at all."

Once she'd moved out of the way and shifted her vehicle into Park, Susannah was able to breathe a sigh of relief. She reached into her designer purse and pulled out the cosmetic bag she'd tossed in at the last minute. Did her lipstick need a touch-up? Was all her armor still fully in place? But as she opened her powder compact and her gaze flitted to the mirror, she knew neither of those things would make a difference. What she wanted most of all in that moment was to feel like the person she was in the inside still matched the glamorous woman who looked back at her in the reflection.

She didn't. *That* Susannah Simmons may as well have been a stranger—a stranger the new Susannah Simmons wasn't even sure she liked very much anymore.

Everything about this feels wrong. Her chest went so tight that she could hardly breathe. She needed to get all that paint off her face...*now.*

She dug around the cosmetic bag until she found a packet of makeup remover wipes and scrubbed until her scar reappeared. Then, as layer after layer of the pancake foundation came off, she spied the rosy glow that she'd recently acquired from all the time she spent outside now that she lived in Emerald Ridge. Her cheeks were sun-kissed, and there was a fresh sprinkle of freckles across the bridge of her nose. Those changes made her smile.

This face might not be able to sell tickets at the box office, but it was still a good face. It belonged to the sort of woman who liked picnics on faded quilts, the feeling of a horse swaying beneath her and the sound of Labrador paws romping on soft pine needles. The sort of woman who'd nearly died but fought her way back from the brink. Above all, the sort of woman who wanted the time she had left on this earth to *matter.*

When Oliver looked at her, he didn't see her scars. He saw her *soul.* He saw her heart. He saw the hopes and dreams she'd had back when she was an innocent fourteen-year-old. No matter what happened between them now, he'd given her the gift of seeing herself that way again, too.

She reached back into the cosmetic bag for a brush.

It only took a second or two to comb out the bombshell style she'd spent hours on earlier and gather her hair into a simple high ponytail. Once the transformation was complete, she could finally breathe again.

That's so much better, she thought as she took in her reflection. *This is who I am now, and it's who I want to be.*

She didn't even want this meeting anymore. She longed for her cozy life here in Emerald Ridge—her dogs, her writing and her ranch.

Most of all, she wanted Oliver.

Susannah tossed the makeup bag back into her purse and grabbed her cell phone. She tapped Brett's contact information and banged out a text. Blunt, brief and, most important, final.

The meeting is off. I never want to see you or Hollywood ever again. I'm blocking your number.

There. She felt better already, like an enormous burden had been lifted from her shoulders—the burden of her old life threatening to swallow her whole again. She could do whatever she wanted now.

Be whomever she chose.

Love without limits.

She closed out the message to Brett and immediately followed through on her promise to block his number before he had a chance to text her back. Then, with trembling hands, she called Oliver.

The phone rang enough times that she thought the

call might roll to voicemail, but just as her newfound optimism began to dim, he picked up.

"Susannah." His tone had that same wooden quality from the night on the deck when she'd asked him how he felt about having children.

Her heart stumbled as she searched for the words to turn everything around and undo the damage from that terrible night. "Oliver, I—"

It didn't matter what she said, though, because he didn't give her a chance to finish.

"Let's not do this, okay?" he said coldly. "Things are over between us, so there's really no reason to drag this out."

Over? That sounded awfully final. Didn't he want to know why she was calling? Their time together in Emerald Ridge had been special, just like the summer when they were kids. She knew it had—not just to her, but to him, too. And now he was going to throw it away without even having an open and honest conversation?

"Oliver, I think there might be some kind of misunderstanding. I—"

"You really don't have to do this, Susannah. I know I've lost you." He still sounded stony, but there was a telltale catch in his voice when he said her name, and it made her die a little bit inside. "Let's just say goodbye and be done with it."

Her head spun. A goodbye was the very last thing she wanted from Oliver, but he'd made up his mind, hadn't he? He'd assumed the very worst of her, and words weren't going to fix it. Not even words like *I love you* or I want forever with you…*right here, right now.*

He hadn't hung up yet, so there was still time. But Susannah didn't have it in her to fight for their future. Not all by herself. It wasn't supposed to be this way. She shouldn't have to beg the man she loved to listen to what she had to say. And she couldn't make him believe in her when he was always bracing for the worst, waiting for proof he'd been lied to.

Even if she could, how long would it last? If he didn't trust her now, maybe he never would.

Blinking back tears, she drew a deep breath and gave him what he thought he wanted. It was the least she could do after all the kindness he'd shown her. He'd saved her as surely as if he'd pulled her broken body from the wreckage. Sadly, he just didn't realize it.

"Goodbye, Oliver."

Chapter Thirteen

Susannah poured her heart into the pages of a new manuscript for the rest of the week. She missed Oliver terribly, but now that she was fully committed to her new life, she wanted to immerse herself in it. For real, this time.

She spent long hours at her computer, punctuated by meandering walks with Hershey, Honey and Bear, and yoga on the back deck. In the evenings, she cooked lavish meals—comfort food like her grandmother used to make. Then she'd curl up on the sofa with Hershey and read a mystery novel until the owls in the woods behind the log house began to hoot, signaling it was time to close her eyes and go to sleep.

Once, she even ventured into town without her disguise. She walked straight into ER Grocery, barefaced, to purchase a bird feeder and wind chimes for the back porch. There'd been a few stares and whispers, but Susannah held her head high and smiled at the other customers. Once she made eye contact, she realized no one was horrified by the way she looked. They wore the same starstruck expression she'd spied on the valet's face a few days ago at the hotel—the look of someone seeing a celebrity in real life. Scars couldn't dim her shine. Only *fear* could do that.

By Saturday, however, she still hadn't made a final decision about Kate Fortune's party. It wasn't being around people that gave her pause, so much as the fact that Oliver would be there.

She didn't know how she was going to face him again. Eventually, she wouldn't have a choice. He was going to be her *neighbor*. Emerald Ridge was a small town, and so far, her limited social circle consisted of her three dogs and the Fortunes. Period. Just yesterday, Madeline called to invite her to a girls' day next week at Coffee Connection, a cozy spot downtown that Susannah had been eyeing every time she drove past it. She'd been grateful for the invitation, especially after Madeline insisted it came with no strings attached. Even if she chose not to attend Kate's party, Madeline wanted to be her friend.

And Susannah needed a friend right now, even if that friend was Oliver's sister.

Whether she went to the party or not, she was going to have to see him. It was a matter of *when*, not *if*.

She wasn't sure she could do it. Acting had always come easy to Susannah. At the best of times, slipping into another life and pretending to be someone else had been fun. Even at the worst of times, it had been a much-needed escape from reality. This was different, though. She couldn't fake anything where Oliver was concerned. He'd hurt her, and there was no pretending otherwise.

But she wasn't angry at him anymore.

Everyone he'd ever loved had betrayed him in some fundamental way, and those kinds of wounds left scars that ran far deeper than the physical ailments she was still dealing with a full year after her accident. She understood how hard it was for him to trust people, and while she still couldn't believe he actually thought she had feelings for Brett, the hurt wasn't as raw and furious as it had been a few days ago. Since then, it had settled into her bones with quiet acceptance and a heartbreak she wasn't sure she'd ever get over. Her relationship with Brett had ended with a spectacular crash, but her feelings for Oliver were, quite simply, *endless*.

"I'm not afraid," she told Hershey the morning of the party. "I'd just rather not go."

The dog tilted his head like he didn't quite believe her.

"Stop looking at me like that. I'm perfectly comfortable in my own skin now. I'm proud of who I am." Mostly, anyway. She didn't need anyone's approval, but she desperately wanted Oliver's. A part of her still wanted to prove to him that she was ready to start a new life with him, even if he hadn't quite caught up.

Could she do it, though? Could she really walk into the Emerald Ridge Hotel and exchange pleasantries with him after everything that had happened over the past few weeks?

Hershey regarded her with that penetrating canine gaze of his, letting her know in no uncertain terms how he felt about it. He missed Oliver, and she knew it. All the dogs did. The way they'd whined at the door following his departure the other night still haunted her.

She'd had to lure them away with chunks of cheddar cheese, and even then, they'd been uncharacteristically quiet. No one touched a squeaky toy for several days afterward.

"Okay, maybe—" she started, but then her phone pinged with a notification, cutting her off.

Susannah strode toward the kitchen island where her device sat plugged into an outlet. She'd left all the tabs open to new recipes she wanted to try this week, but when she picked it up, there wasn't a mouthwatering photo of banana pudding or peach pie on the tiny screen. Instead, she found herself looking at an email… *the* email. The literary agent she'd completely given up on days ago had finally sent her a message.

Susannah gasped, and the Labradors gathered round, ears pricked forward in curiosity. She read the email out loud even though they couldn't fully understand. Surely they could tell by her tone that it was good news.

"Dear Miss Simmons, it was such a delight to hear from you. While I'd still love to discuss a memoir if you ever decide to share your story, I'm equally thrilled you've turned your talents to fiction. Apologies for the delay in getting back to you… I wanted to give your manuscript my full attention. To be frank, I find most celebrity fiction in heavy need of a ghostwriter. I'm pleased to say that yours is the rare exception. You have a remarkable talent for storytelling! I'm confident I can find the right publisher for your mystery novel debut—it has all the makings of a breakout title. Let's set up a time to talk next steps."

She read the entire thing without taking a breath,

hands shaking as she gripped her phone. Finally, some good news. Not just good, but *great*. Her writing dreams were going to come true. All her life, she'd dreamed of becoming a mystery author, and it was finally happening!

Aside from her dogs, there was only one person in the entire world she wanted to share the news with. One person who would understand how much it meant to her and whose opinion mattered more than all the others.

Hershey, Honey and Bear wagged their excitement as she smiled to herself and clutched her phone to her chest.

Looks like I'm going to that party, after all.

The ballroom of the Emerald Ridge Hotel shimmered like a storybook. Madeline had really outdone herself. Susannah had been to A-list parties all over the world—the film festival in Cannes, the annual fashion gala at the Metropolitan Museum in New York, the Governors Ball after the Academy Awards ceremony—but the elegant scene Madeline had created for Kate Fortune's one-hundredth birthday party was luxurious enough to rival them all. .

Waiters in crisp white jackets moved like clockwork, offering trays of hors d'oeuvres and bubbling drinks. A string quartet played softly from the corner, their soothing notes floating beneath the cheerful hum of conversation and laughter. Everything gleamed with warmth and opulence, a perfect blend of old-money grandeur and Madeline's signature touch of modern glamour.

Susannah paused just inside the entrance, taking a deep breath.

She'd been so determined to stay away tonight. But she was here now, and like her other recent forays into town, she wore no scarf, no shawl, no carefully tilted hat. The scar that ran from just beneath her left eye down toward her jaw was certainly visible in the soft ballroom lighting.

Still, she pushed her shoulders back and stood up straight.

No more hiding, she reminded herself.

"Susannah?"

She turned toward the voice and barely had time to smile before Madeline Fortune swept her into a hug.

"You're here!" The lovely redhead pulled back and blinked rapidly, her hands gripping Susannah's arms as if to make sure she was real. "Oh my word. You really came."

"I said I might," Susannah said softly, "but I wasn't sure I'd actually walk through the door."

Madeline shook her head, beaming through tears. "And just look at you. You're radiant, Susannah. Absolutely radiant."

Susannah's throat tightened. She hadn't expected that. Not the way Madeline said it, as though she truly meant it.

She smiled, her voice thick. "I figured if I was going to show up for Kate, I should show up all the way."

Madeline's eyes glistened. "You have no idea what

this is going to mean to her. She's been asking about you all night. Come on… She's just through here."

The two women wove their way through the throng of partygoers, and Susannah let people look. She didn't duck her head or turn away. A few glances lingered—some curious, some surprised—but more than one person offered her a warm nod or small, respectful smile.

She could do this…for Kate.

And for Oliver.

They reached a pair of tall double doors, and just before Madeline pulled her inside, Susannah searched the room for his familiar thick, dark hair, wide shoulders and the crooked smile she loved so much. She couldn't find him, though.

Surely he's coming, she thought. Then, as her worry took root and her hands began to tremble, she sent up a silent prayer. *Please, please let him be here.*

"Kate, I hope you're ready for a big birthday surprise!" Madeline said in a singsong voice.

She ushered Susannah inside a quiet sitting room lit by soft lamplight, close enough to the hustle and bustle of the main party in the ballroom to feel festive, but with an elevated privacy that gave off a distinctly regal air—even though Kate Fortune wasn't technically royalty.

She was *Texas* royalty.

Still, the elder woman didn't need a crown or a Happy Birthday sash to make her the center of attention. Her perfect posture, even at one hundred years old, coupled with her elegant mannerisms, left no doubt who this celebration was for.

A martini glass rested in her hands, the clear liquid inside untouched, as if she'd been too busy holding court to take a single sip. The people she'd been chatting with slipped past Susannah as they exited the room just as Kate looked up—and froze.

A lump sprang to Susannah's throat as their eyes met. She hadn't expected to get so emotional, but with one look, the years between them slipped away and a single, startling revelation washed over her.

Kate was the closest thing to a mother or a grandmother that she had left. She hadn't thought of it that way before. Until Madeline had reached out about the party, she'd been convinced Kate didn't even remember her. But that clearly wasn't the case.

The older woman rose slowly, with the help of a pearl-studded cane, her eyes never leaving Susannah's face. For a long beat, no one said a word.

Then Kate's voice, thin but fierce, broke the hush. "Susannah? Is that really you?"

"It's me." She nodded.

Madeline stepped aside, giving them space. Susannah reached for Kate's hands and let the older woman cup her cheeks.

"My dear girl," Kate whispered. "You came."

Susannah blinked hard, but a tear slipped loose anyway. "Happy birthday, Aunt Kate."

Kate smiled. She still wore the same signature red lipstick Susannah remembered so well, and suddenly she felt herself wrapped up in a familiar cloud of perfume. What was the scent she'd loved so much back in the day?

Chanel No. 5. Susannah grinned as she thought about the white porcelain container of dusting powder Kate had always kept on her dressing table. Gold interlocking C's topped the lid, and inside, a soft white puff rested atop the fragrant powder. Susannah had never seen anything so glamorous in her entire life.

"You beautiful thing. This is all I wanted for my birthday. All I prayed for. Just to see your face again…" Kate spoke with a reverence that carried the full weight of those words.

Kate Fortune wasn't known for softness. She was sharp-witted, silver-tongued and as formidable as the empire her family had built. But in that moment, her voice held none of its usual steel.

"I wasn't sure I could," Susannah confessed. "Not like this."

She lifted a hand to indicate her scar, and Kate simply reached out and gently caught it midair, guiding it down with a firm but loving touch.

"You are exactly how you are meant to be," she said with a wag of her finger. "There's still so much ahead for you."

"I'm starting to understand that." Susannah nodded. "It took me a while, but I'm getting there."

Kate's eyes twinkled. "That's all right, darling. I took a hundred years to get here myself."

Chapter Fourteen

Oliver had never been less in the mood for a party as he was on the night of Kate Fortune's big birthday celebration. Staying holed up in his room or hiding out at the ranch weren't viable options, however. He'd given Madeline his word that he'd be there. Besides, he was a Fortune now, and from all appearances as he glanced around the hotel ballroom, there wasn't a Fortune in the entire Lone Star state who hadn't turned out for the big event.

The royal branch of the family that the entire town had been whispering about had indeed turned up, as had the Fortunes of Red Rock. In fact, because his sister thought of everything, Madeline had arranged for the party to be catered by the Mexican restaurant Red, based in Red Rock, Texas, and owned by the Mendoza family. From what Oliver had heard, so many Mendozas had married Fortunes over the years that the two Texas dynasties were practically one and the same.

Oliver moved through the room in his Western tuxedo—crisp white shirt, black jacket with a front-and-back-corded yoke, etched-bone buttons and smooth-satin lapel, paired with a Western crossover tie and polished cowboy boots in black ostrich leather. He grabbed a champagne flute as one of the servers moved past him with a tray of sparkling glasses, just to give himself something to do with his hands. While sipping, he made small talk with a few Fortunes from a rural town called Rambling Rose and listened as Jerome Fortune reminisced about attending Kate Fortune's ninetieth birthday party ten years ago. Mostly, he marveled at the sheer size of his newly discovered extended family and did his best to pretend he wanted to be there when his heart was someplace else entirely.

She's moved on, he reminded himself every time the temptation to call Susannah hit him hard in the chest.

He was convinced he'd done the right thing, no matter how painful it had been. Still, he couldn't seem to let go of something she'd started to say during that last phone call the other day.

Oliver, I think there might be some kind of misunderstanding...

The truth was, even if he'd made a mistake and jumped to conclusions about her and Brett, she was still better off without him. Oliver knew that now. There was something broken inside him that simply couldn't be fixed. He'd never be able to make Susannah happy—not in the way she deserved.

Brett had made his intentions clear. He'd come blazing into town intent on sweeping her off her feet, if the rumors Oliver heard swirling around the hotel were to be believed. By comparison, what had *he* done to prove how badly he cared for her? Nothing. He'd run.

How did that make him any better than that slick Hollywood jerk?

It didn't.

"Where did you say your branch of the family is from again?" Madeline asked a tall fella in a black cowboy hat as she winked at Oliver without missing a beat.

"Chatelaine, Texas," the man—who'd introduced himself to Oliver earlier as West Fortune—said. "It's an old mining town. We've got one gas station with a single pump, so technically Chatelaine is home to more Fortunes than fuel nozzles. But we've got plenty of grit."

Madeline laughed, and Oliver figured he should join the conversation. Brooding in a dark corner wasn't going to make the evening pass any faster. He might need to make some kind of annotated flow chart to keep track of the family tree, though.

By the time he sidled up next to Madeline, West Fortune had moved on, which was just as well. He'd hoped to have a word in private with his sister, which seemed like a pipe dream since the ballroom was filled to capacity.

"Cheers to you, Mads." He held up his glass. "You pulled off the party of the century."

"You mean the party of *Kate's* century." She grinned as she tapped her champagne flute against his. "Have you had a chance to meet the guest of honor yet?"

He shook his head. "Not yet."

"She said something earlier about wanting to talk to all of Archibald's children together. *Tonight*. She was pretty adamant, so I'm sure you'll get your chance sooner rather than later," his sister said.

Oliver frowned into his glass of bubbly. "That sounds mysterious."

He didn't need any more mystery in his life, thank you very much. He'd come to Emerald Ridge looking for answers about his mom, and he'd found way, *way* more than he'd bargained for.

It hadn't been all bad, however. He'd found a home here, along with the siblings he'd always longed for back when he'd been growing up an only child. For a while, he'd even found love.

"Madeline, I'm sorry Susannah chose not to come tonight." He wished he could say it was anyone's fault but his. "That's on me, I'm afraid. I hate that Kate is going to be disappointed. I just hope she doesn't blame you. You did your best."

Madeline's flute paused halfway to her lips. She shot him a curious glance. "What are you talking about?"

"I…um…" Oliver swallowed around the boulder lodged in his throat. He hadn't planned on talking about everything that had gone wrong between the two of them. He'd simply wanted to apologize and move on. "Let's just say we're not seeing each other anymore and leave it at that."

"If that's true, then I'm sure it *is* your fault, because Susannah is perfectly lovely. I'm going to need a full debrief on that when we aren't surrounded by two hundred of Kate Fortune's nearest and dearest. But that's not what I meant. Susannah shared a lovely reunion with Kate just a few minutes ago. She's here at the party." Madeline's gaze flitted somewhere over his right shoulder. "Right over there, as a matter of fact."

Oliver's heart stuttered. He turned slowly, as if moving too fast might make the moment vanish.

There, across the ballroom, stood Susannah.

She wasn't looking at him now—she was smiling politely at someone he couldn't see, her posture graceful, her lush blond waves swept to one side in a simple side ponytail. Unlike at the toddler party, she wasn't hiding behind a curtain of hair or trying to disguise herself with makeup or a hat. Tonight, she wore a silver satin evening gown that shimmered with every step, the delicate fabric catching the light and flowing over her figure like liquid mercury. There was nothing flashy about it. No sequins or dramatic neckline, just stunning simplicity and quiet confidence.

She looked like herself, not Susannah Simmons the movie star. The scar on her cheek was barely noticeable beneath the soft glow of the chandeliers, or maybe he'd simply gotten used to it. It was a part of her now, and every part of her still had the power to undo him. This was the Suzy he'd met all those years ago, but now she was all grown up and just like he remembered—composed, radiant, effortlessly beautiful.

And entirely out of reach.

He'd been so sure she wouldn't come. That he'd ruined any chance of seeing her again, let alone making things right.

Madeline bumped her shoulder lightly against his. "You okay?"

No. Not even a little.

But he nodded anyway, unable to tear his gaze away from Susannah. "Yeah. I just wasn't expecting to see her."

Because if he'd known she was coming, he would've braced for impact. Her eyes met his, steady and unreadable, and in that instant, the room faded. The music, the laughter, the soft clinking of glasses—all of it vanished beneath the weight of that single glance.

He didn't know what he expected to see in her expression. Anger? Hurt? Indifference? But what he saw was worse. It was kindness. Calm, quiet *kindness*.

And it unraveled him completely.

"I'll let you two talk." Madeline gave his elbow a squeeze. "Just remember what I said the other day, okay? Tell her how you feel. If you don't, she'll never know."

Oliver nodded, but that was easier said than done, wasn't it? Especially when he didn't *want* to feel anything, because lately he'd begun to realize some things about himself that he didn't like.

At all.

He tightened his grip on his champagne flute and made his way toward Susannah without any idea of what he was going to say. She made it easy for him, though, because that's who Susannah was. She handled even the most awkward circumstances with grace.

"Hi there." She offered him a fleeting smile. Tentative and uncertain. It did little to ease the raw ache that had hollowed out his chest ever since he'd overheard the gossip about her and Brett in the hotel lobby.

"Hey. It's great to see you here. I know Madeline

is thrilled you decided to come." He swallowed hard. "She's not the only one."

"Really?" Susannah asked.

It killed him that she had to ask, but he knew he only had himself to blame. "Really."

"I didn't just come for Madeline and Kate. I wanted to see you, Oliver." Her voice trembled. She bit her bottom lip and took a deep breath. "I have so much I want to say, but now that I'm standing here in front of you, I don't know where to start."

"Start anywhere," he said gently. "I'll listen this time."

He *should* have listened to her before. Was it too late?

"Will you really?"

His throat tightened. "I promise. Every word."

"I'm not sure what you heard, but I'm not with Brett. I never was, not even for a minute. In fact, he came all the way down here to talk about a Hollywood comeback, and I didn't even show up for the meeting," she confided, and he could tell how wrong he'd been about her and Brett just by the look in her eyes. She didn't feel anything for her ex. She never had. "I told him I would, but when I got here on the morning of our meeting, I couldn't get out of the car. It just didn't feel right. Going back to that life isn't what I want. It never was."

She drew herself up a little, her chin tilting with quiet resolve. "And for the record, you don't get to assume the worst about me and then expect me to come running just because you finally decided to listen. I came here because I needed to say my piece, not because I owe you an explanation."

The words stung, but she didn't hesitate. This time, she was the one holding her ground.

Shame wound into a tight sickening knot in Oliver's chest. There'd never been a romantic rendezvous. All that time, Brett had been preparing for a business meeting— a meeting Susannah had never even attended. The roses, the Cristal, the imported truffles... None of them had meant a thing.

How had he let himself believe she'd go back to the man who'd left her bruised and broken? She'd told him how she felt all along, and somehow he'd convinced himself she'd been lying.

Because that's what people did. They lied. And Oliver was sick of it. He'd been so intent on not letting the rug get pulled out from under him again that he'd yanked it out himself.

Going back to that life isn't what I want. It never was.

He held on to those words like they were a lifeline. He desperately wanted to ask her what she *did* want, but he no longer had that right, did he? He'd thrown it away when he'd pressed her into saying goodbye.

"I'm sorry," he said hoarsely.

Sorry I lost faith in you...sorry I lost faith in us. So very sorry.

"We don't have to talk about Brett anymore, Oliver. In fact, I'd be perfectly happy if I never heard his name again. Besides, that's not why I wanted to see you." She smiled again, and this time it reached her eyes, as bright as the summer sunshine. "I heard back from the literary agent today. Just a little bit ago, in fact. She thinks she can sell my book. It's really happening. I'm going to be a mystery author."

Without warning, she threw her arms around him, and suddenly it was all too much—her softness, her familiar strawberries-and-cream scent, the way she fit so perfectly against him. He squeezed his eyes shut tight and did his best to memorize how it felt to hold her again.

When she finally pulled back, he smiled at her. "Well, look at you, Nancy Drew. Congratulations. You deserve this, Suzy Q. You really do."

Maybe it was hearing her call him Suzy Q again, that nickname only he had ever used. Or maybe the sudden embrace had rocked her as much as it did him. Whatever it was, something shifted…something old and familiar cracked wide-open between them. Then she looked up at him, eyes shining, bottom lip trembling just slightly, and he knew—he just *knew*—that whatever she was about to say was going to wreck him all over again.

"I love you, Oliver," she whispered.

His heart stalled in his chest.

"I didn't plan on saying that tonight." She let out a tiny laugh as she glanced around at the well-dressed party guests, the string quartet tucked in the corner, the floral arrangements overflowing with fresh peonies. "I know it's not the right time or place, but I just can't hold it in anymore. I want us to be together. I want us to build a life. A *family*. Right here in Emerald Ridge, the place we both love so much."

Oliver felt the air leave his lungs like he'd taken a punch to the chest.

For days, he'd been replaying that last phone call in his head, wishing he could take it all back. Wishing he'd trusted what they had instead of letting fear drive him away.

And now here she was, in the middle of a ballroom filled with strangers and champagne and sweet second chances, telling him she still loved him. That she wanted a life and a family. With *him*.

He didn't deserve her. He probably never had. But oh, how he wanted her anyway.

She went on, voice steadier now, words tumbling from her lips before she could stop them. "I know things between us are complicated, and I realize you might not want the same things I do, but I had to tell you while I had the chance."

While I had the chance.

Because he'd forced her into a goodbye that neither one of them really wanted. There was clearly something very wrong with him. Something he wasn't sure he could ever fix.

"I do want those things," he said, and the hollow ache in his tone was unmistakable, even to his own ears. "But…"

He wanted to believe her. He really did, but his heart was still battered and bruised from thinking she'd gone back to her old life. He'd closed up so tight afterward that he wasn't sure how to open himself up again.

"But?" Susannah prompted as her smile died on her lips.

Oliver didn't even know what to say, didn't know what to do. All he knew was that he felt like he might be turning into his father. Archibald Fortune had been too guarded to love anyone the way they truly deserved. That had been the long and short of it. He'd given himself to everyone and no one, all at the same time.

And now here Oliver stood, on the verge of following in those very questionable footsteps. Not as a polygamist, obviously, but as a man who couldn't… *wouldn't*…ever allow anyone to truly know himself.

Was that really what he wanted?

"Oliver, here you are. I've been looking for you everywhere," Shelby said, as she swept into their private little orbit in a whirl of tulle and sequins. His sister had been a beauty queen before starting her own business, and she still carried herself with an elegance that made Oliver picture an imaginary tiara on her head every time he saw her.

Shelby's gaze flitted back and forth between Oliver and Susannah. "I hope I'm not interrupting anything."

Oliver let out a quiet cough. "Actually, Susannah and I were…"

Shelby either didn't seem to hear him or chose not to. She barreled ahead with the same unstoppable sparkle that had probably won her a dozen crowns.

"It's just that we're all waiting for you. Kate asked to see all of Archibald's children, and I've managed to round up everyone but you so far." Shelby aimed a pageant-perfect smile at Susannah. "Is it okay if I steal my brother away for a little bit? I promise to bring him back as soon as we're finished."

Susannah gave a gracious nod, even as her eyes flicked toward Oliver. "Of course. Family comes first."

He hesitated, torn between the pull of obligation and the aching need to stay, to finish what had finally started unraveling between them.

"Can we—" he started, then shook his head, trying again. "Will you still be here later?"

She gave him the smallest of smiles but there was a hint of weariness behind it this time, like he'd hurt her too many times in the same exact way. "I'm not going anywhere."

That simple promise, gentle and steady, landed like a pebble dropped in the middle of his chest.

He nodded, grateful and miserable all at once. "Then maybe we can actually talk."

Her gaze flickered, equal parts hope and self-protection. She hesitated, glancing briefly toward his sister before meeting his eyes again.

"Just please don't make promises you can't keep," she said softly—quiet enough to sound polite, but with an edge that told him she wasn't offering blind faith this time.

He swallowed hard, realizing she wasn't offering him an easy way back. She was giving him one last chance to show her he deserved it.

Beside him, Shelby shifted, clearly sensing the tension but pretending not to. The moment hung, fragile and unfinished, until she stepped in to break it.

"Come on, Ollie." Shelby looped her arm through

his with practiced ease. "You're not the long-lost heir anymore. You're *one of us*, and we can't start without you."

Those words, which he'd once craved, barely landed in his consciousness. He couldn't think straight until he got things settled with Susannah, for better or worse.

As Shelby guided him away, Oliver glanced over his shoulder, catching one last glimpse of Susannah standing alone in the soft glow of the chandelier light. Suddenly, without warning, he pictured her waiting at the altar in a flowing white dress with a bouquet of daisies in her hands. Her dogs surrounded her, their thick necks circled with flower wreaths.

For better or worse.

Oliver could see her as a bride. *His* bride. The real question was…

Would she ever let him?

Chapter Fifteen

Shelby led Oliver to a private sitting room situated just outside the entrance to the ballroom, and the ornate double doors closed with a soft click behind them. Inside, the rest of their siblings—Jillian, Hayes, Penn and Madeline—stood shoulder to shoulder, flanked by the three mothers who hovered off to the side.

The first thing Oliver noticed was the eerie hush that fell over the room. It was hard to believe that a glittering black-tie party was still taking place just a few feet away. The second thing he noticed about the gold-lit space was that it smelled faintly of roses and old money.

His gaze veered toward the settee where an older woman—Kate Fortune, he presumed—sat, poised and radiant in a deep plum gown. A jeweled comb held back one side of her silver hair. It was difficult to believe he was looking at someone who'd just turned one hundred years old. Maybe one of the Fortunes in the room next door had stumbled upon the fountain of youth.

"You must be Oliver," she said as she looked him

up and down. She extended a hand toward him, but remained seated. "I'm Kate Fortune."

"Sorry to have kept you waiting." He gave her hand a gentle shake. "Happy birthday, ma'am."

He winked, and her formidable expression cracked slightly, just enough for a hint of amusement to shine through.

"Charming," she said. "Clearly you get that from your father."

"I'm not sure if that's a good thing or a bad one, given the circumstances," Oliver responded with a glance at the others.

"Take the compliment, son. Archibald wasn't all bad." Kate gathered her hands in her lap. Large gemstones sparkled on most of her fingers, casting a kaleidoscope across the silk of her gown.

"He wasn't perfect," she went on, "but none of us are. And in his own way, your father was extraordinary."

The room went still. Even Taffy, who was usually ready with a sardonic quip, remained quiet.

Kate looked around at them all, nine lives bound by one complicated man—six children and three wives. As weird as it seemed, Oliver wished his mother could be there, too. She was just as much a part of this as the rest of them were.

"I want to tell you a story that none of you have heard before. I think it's important for all of you to know something about Archibald that will make you proud. The things that have come to light about your father since his passing have been difficult to hear, but this story is about the beginning, not the end," the older woman said, eyes glittering in the soft light of the sitting room.

The siblings exchanged glances. Oliver slid his hands into his trouser pockets, unsure what to expect. He hoped it wasn't another bombshell family surprise. He still hadn't recovered from the last one.

"Very well, then." Kate drew in a breath and appeared to steady herself. "When I first met your father, he was eighteen years old. Just a boy, really. Bold and skinny, with a chipped tooth and too much charm for his own good. He showed up at my office uninvited and said he'd read about me and my cosmetics empire in a glossy magazine. My assistant kept him waiting, thinking he'd eventually give up and go away. He didn't. He hung around for hours, hoping for a chance to talk to me."

Beside Oliver, Shelby shook her head. "Hold on—he just walked in off the street?"

Kate nodded. "He sure did. When he read that we shared a last name, he wondered if we might be distant relatives. Archibald told me that since his daddy had been disinherited and shunned by his grandfather, he'd never had contact with the rest of the family. Your father never knew a single Fortune growing up, but something in him wanted to change that."

Penn narrowed his gaze at the older woman. "And you believed him? Just like that?"

"Like I said, your father was quite the charmer." Kate arched an eyebrow in the direction of Archibald's wives.

Taffy snorted and Agatha dabbed at the corners of her eyes, while Damaris kept a polite smile fixed in place.

"So then what happened?" Hayes asked.

"He explained that he came from a poor branch of the family and told me a little bit about how he'd been on his own for years already. But it was clear right from the start that he didn't want my pity. He was determined to make something of himself." Kate's rings caught the light again as she reached for her glass of water but didn't drink. "That skinny teenager stood across from me in his threadbare shirt and worn-out jeans and said he wanted to start his own airline. 'So I can fly away whenever I want,' he told me. 'So I never have to stay somewhere I'm not wanted.'"

Oliver blinked, the words hitting somewhere deep in his chest.

"He wanted to control his own destiny. That was the most important thing to him, and after everything he'd gone through in his young life, I understood. I believed him when he told me he would make something of himself someday." Kate shrugged. "He knew it, too. That's why he dared to ask me if I would be willing to invest in him financially."

"Bold," Madeline murmured.

"He was," Kate agreed, a hint of fondness in her tone.

Hayes let out a low whistle. "Begging for charity doesn't sound at all like our dad."

"He wasn't begging," the older woman said sharply.

"He was proud. But he was also brave enough to ask. And determined enough to prove himself."

"So did you do it?" Jillian asked, wide-eyed. "Did you give our dad the money to start Fortune Air?"

Kate held up a single, bony finger. "I gave him one thousand dollars. Just a single check. I told him there wouldn't be another, and if he really was who he claimed to be—a Fortune in blood and ambition—he'd make it stretch. He'd use it to build that airline he talked about. Every business starts with one small seed, and that's what I gave him. *A seed.*"

She paused, her voice softening. "And that's exactly what he did. He took the seed I offered him, and he nurtured it until it blossomed beyond anything he could've hoped for. Your father built Fortune Air all on his own. The investment I made was just a little something to let him know someone believed in him. Someone cared. Sometimes that's all it takes to give someone the confidence to follow through on their dreams."

A few of Oliver's sisters began to sniffle. He was beginning to feel misty-eyed himself.

"Did you ever hear from him again?" Hayes asked in a voice gruff with emotion.

"I certainly did," Kate said with a nod. Her blue eyes had gone watery, and they glistened like dark sapphires. "Every year, on the anniversary of the day he started Fortune Air, Archibald sent me a thank-you card. He never missed a single one. Not even this past year."

"So you heard from him recently, then?" Agatha

asked. "Fortune Air's anniversary wasn't too long before he passed away."

Oliver's heart went out to her, the first of Archibald's wives. Here was yet another secret that he apparently hadn't shared with her. She seemed as surprised by Kate Fortune's story as the rest of them were.

Agatha held her head high, though. The wounds from her husband's betrayal weren't as fresh as they'd been a few months ago. Stories like this one reminded them all that Archibald Fortune was only human. Oliver was glad they'd all had a chance to read through his journal first. Knowing about his hardships made what Kate was telling them all the more remarkable.

His feelings for his dad were still complicated. They probably always would be, but he was glad Archibald had found someone to believe in him. Everyone needed someone like Kate Fortune in their lives. For Oliver, that person had always been his mother.

He drew in a shaky breath, realizing he'd been awfully hard on his mom's memory since discovering the truth about his past. Sure, he still wished she'd told him about his father, but now he truly understood that she had her reasons for taking that secret to the grave. In her own way, she'd been protecting him. Despite the name changes, the lies and the questions she'd never fully answered, she had loved him. That much was undeniable.

She'd simply been doing her best. In a way, so had Archibald. They'd both left their share of messes in their wake, but that was life, wasn't it? Messy…chaotic. But that didn't mean it couldn't be beautiful.

"Archibald reached out to me just a few months before he passed. He wrote to me on the airline's anniversary, just like clockwork." Kate reached into the slim beaded clutch tucked beside her on the settee.

The siblings exchanged glances as she pulled out a pale blue envelope.

"Given the timing of this letter, I thought you all might be interested in reading it." Kate arched a perfectly manicured eyebrow at Madeline. "Especially you, darling Madeline."

His sister's hand fluttered to her throat as her cheeks flared pink. "Me?"

Kate offered her the envelope. "Why don't you read it aloud to everyone, and then you'll see."

Madeline cast a questioning glance at Oliver. He wasn't sure why she'd singled him out for encouragement, but it warmed his heart in a way that made him think maybe he wasn't as hopeless as he'd thought. He liked being a big brother, and he liked the closeness that had begun to develop between them. If he could trust his innermost thoughts and feelings with a sister, maybe he could trust them with someone else someday...

Maybe even sooner than he realized.

A small smile tugged at his mouth as he offered Madeline a quiet nod.

She took a deep breath and slid a robin's-egg blue slip of paper from the envelope. Then she slowly unfolded the letter with a reverence Oliver could feel clear across the room.

The paper shook slightly in Madeline's hands as

she cleared her throat and began to read. "'Dear Kate, Fortune Air is another year older, and as always, I'm eternally grateful for your encouragement. You gave me wings when I couldn't even afford a compass. I owe you more than a thank-you, but I've always believed gratitude should be consistent and heartfelt. So here it is again—thank you for believing in me.'"

Madeline's smile wobbled as she glanced up at Kate.

"Go on, darling." The older woman flicked a hand in the air, and the diamond bangle bracelets on her wrist tinkled like bells. "The best is yet to come."

The best is yet to come. Oliver sure hoped that was true, not just for Madeline, but for every last Fortune in this room. If anyone was capable of bringing a sense of real closure to their family, it seemed like Kate would be up to the task. She'd held them all spellbound since the moment she'd begun speaking.

His sister glanced back down at the letter, eyes wide as she read the next part so quickly that her tongue tripped over the words. "'I heard you're turning one hundred years old this year. Congratulations on a century well lived. A life like yours deserves a proper celebration. If you're looking for a party planner, my daughter Madeline's the best in the business.'"

She gasped, and her hand flew to her mouth. "*This* is why you called and asked me to plan your party?"

Kate nodded as she tucked a strand of silver hair behind her ear. "As usual, your father simply wouldn't take no for an answer. He followed up his letter with a phone call. Said he wanted to make absolutely sure I knew how much that first thousand had meant to him.

Archibald didn't normally call—he usually let his annual thank-you card speak for itself. So when he mentioned you again and insisted you'd plan the perfect one-hundredth birthday celebration, I knew he meant business."

Madeline clutched the letter to her chest. "A while back, you said that he'd given you a referral for my business, but I never imagined something like this… That the entire party was his idea, or that he'd been so persistent. He never told me."

"Maybe he wanted to surprise you." Kate winked. "Or maybe he knew it would matter more if it came from me. You can keep the letter if you like, darling."

"I'd like that very much." Madeline's voice caught as she refolded the letter and pressed it to her heart again. "Thank you. This means so much to me."

A stillness settled over the room. No one seemed to breathe until Shelby reached for Madeline's free hand and gave it a squeeze. Madeline glanced up at her sister, and then hugged her so tight that Oliver could hear the breath hitch in Shelby's throat. Then Madeline let go, and one by one, she embraced each of them in turn, until her happiness became theirs. Shared joy…shared healing. Like Kate Fortune's story and the letter written in their father's hand were the final threads stitching them all together. At last.

Oliver swallowed, but the emotion pressing against his throat held firm, unmoved. "I didn't realize Archibald had that in him."

In the beginning, it had been so easy to think of Archibald Fortune as selfish. Evil, even. Reading the journal and learning about his brokenness had made him seem human. But hearing Madeline read his letter to Kate had finally made Oliver see him as something else…

A father.

Oliver had lived all his life without a dad. He'd come to terms with it a long, long time ago. Or so he'd thought. But thinking of Archibald as an actual father figure for the first time sent a wave of grief crashing over him the likes of which he'd never experienced before.

"He had a lot in him, Oliver. Not just the broken parts that led him to some very questionable choices, but good things, too. Hopes…dreams…" Kate kept her gaze trained on him throughout what felt like an intentional pause. "Love."

Oliver's jaw tensed. *He had an awfully strange way of showing it.*

In the past few weeks, he'd gone from quietly despising his father to pitying him. Now, he just wanted to stop thinking about him long enough to get his equilibrium back. He'd never even met the man. Letting go of him should've been easy.

But it wasn't.

Because somewhere between the lines of Archibald's journal and the tremble in Kate's voice as she read that letter, Oliver had started to *feel* him.

"He didn't always know how to give it or show it. That's why I wanted you to hear this from me. Not the headlines, not the scandal. The truth. Your father loved all six of you very much," Kate said, but her eyes remained glued to Oliver, as if she somehow knew he was the one who needed to hear it the most.

All six of us, Oliver thought with an ache deep in the center of his chest.

He really and truly was one of them now, wasn't he? Not just a Fortune by birth, by blood or by name. But by heart.

A dry huff came from the back of the room, and all heads swiveled in unison toward Taffy.

"He drove me nuts," she admitted. "I told you a while back that I was tired of being angry at him, but I'm still not sure I can completely forgive him. But maybe I can forgive him…fifty percent?"

Everyone chuckled, quietly at first, then with a little more ease, as if the tension in the room had finally exhaled right along with them.

"Did I really just say that?" Taffy blinked, clearly startled by her own words.

Madeline bit back a smile and said, "Yes, and I wish I had it on video."

Taffy shot her daughter a look. "Don't push your luck."

But the corner of her mouth twitched, betraying the affection behind her usual sharpness.

Oliver found himself smiling, just barely, and when he glanced around the room—at Kate, at Madeline, at every face that had slowly, reluctantly come to mean something to him—he realized the ache in his chest hadn't gone away.

But it didn't feel quite so heavy anymore. For the

first time in a long time, maybe ever, he didn't feel like a visitor in someone else's family story.

He was part of it now.

And ready or not, he wasn't alone.

Chapter Sixteen

"**S**hall we get back to the party?" Madeline checked the time on the sleek gold watch strapped around her slender wrist and glanced at Kate. "The fireworks are going to be starting soon."

Oliver raised his eyebrows in stunned appreciation. There were *fireworks*? He had to hand it to Madeline. Archibald had been right—she'd been the perfect party planner for Kate Fortune's one-hundredth birthday celebration.

"That sounds lovely." The guest of honor rose from the settee, leaning heavily on her pearl-studded glossy black walking cane, which was topped with an intricately carved gold rose. The center of the flower was topped with a large, lustrous pearl, and there was zero doubt in Oliver's mind that it was the real deal. "I'm nearly ready to call it a night. I'm not ninety-five anymore, you know."

Oliver stifled a grin. He would've liked to see Kate Fortune at ninety-five. She was sharp and formidable at one hundred. He couldn't imagine what she'd been like five years younger.

He stepped forward to offer the older woman his arm. "May I escort you to the balcony?"

She eyed his elbow with a frown. "I may not be ninety-five, but I can still walk myself outside to watch a fireworks display, young man."

"My apologies, ma'am." He laughed softly and bowed his head.

When he looked up again, he found Kate watching him with the same sparkle in her eye that she'd had when she'd been reminiscing about Archibald. "I was right about you. You *are* a charmer."

"See you at next year's celebration when you turn one hundred and one?"

He winked at her, and a faint pink bloomed across Kate's papery cheeks. She lifted her chin, gaze shimmering with quiet delight. Clearly, the passage of time hadn't dulled her pride, nor had it made her immune to flattery.

"I'd like that very much," she said. Then her gaze shifted toward the door to the private sitting room as it swished open, and her expression immediately glazed over.

"Well," she muttered in a tone as dry as dust. "I don't recall Huey, Dewey and Louie being on the guest list. Your sister must've invited them."

Oliver followed her gaze and spotted the triplet attorneys who'd been handling Archibald's estate. He laughed under his breath. "Not a fan of lawyers?"

She rolled her eyes. "Darling, I'm a century old now. The only briefs I'm interested in are the ones in those saucy Calvin Klein advertisements, not the legal sort."

"Fair enough," Oliver said with a chuckle.

She reached up to cup his face with one of her fragile hands, her touch surprisingly gentle as she patted his cheek. "Until next time, Oliver Fortune."

"Until next time, ma'am," he echoed, and he hoped there'd really be a next time. He had a feeling that Kate had plenty more stories left to tell. "Happy birthday."

The elder woman grinned, a flicker of warmth crossing her features. "Thank you, dear. Now I'm off to enjoy my party. I'm not getting any younger, you know."

With a graceful nod, she turned on her heel and made her way toward the exit, deftly sidestepping the triplet attorneys.

The three men stood just inside the door, their expressions a mix of professional and apologetic.

"Sorry to interrupt the celebration," one of them began, clearing his throat. "We have some news regarding Archibald's estate, and we knew the entire family would be in attendance this evening."

Oliver's gaze darted from one triplet to the next. He was always getting them mixed up. How anyone managed to keep them straight was a mystery as big as Texas.

"What now?" Taffy said dryly. "Let me guess… You're here to tell us that Archibald had a fourth secret family."

"Mom," Madeline whispered. "Honestly. You're impossible."

"It was just a joke, honey. I'm not bitter anymore, remember?" Taffy shrugged and glanced around at the others. "Too soon?"

"Way too soon," Hayes said, but the smirk on his face was one of amusement, not irritation.

"Archibald Fortune wouldn't have been Archibald Fortune without one last twist." Penn gave a playful shrug. "I could maybe get on board with a fourth family."

He was joking, obviously. At least they could all laugh about it now.

Oliver snorted lightly and once again glanced between the triplets, who stood looking mildly uncomfortable in their perfectly pressed tuxedos. They probably weren't sure what to make of the united front the nine Fortunes had formed. It had taken a while to get here, after all.

"Well, since you asked," the attorney on the left began, clearing his throat, "there's an update on the estate that requires everyone's immediate attention."

Taffy folded her arms, eyebrow raised. "This better not be another surprise bill."

The lawyer in the middle held up his hands. "No, nothing like that. It's good news, actually."

"News worthy of a splendid celebration like this one," the third triplet added with a nod toward the door.

Oliver wondered how long they had until the fireworks were scheduled to start. He hadn't realized the meeting with Kate would take so long. Nor had he expected to be required to attend a spontaneous legal summit. How long would Susannah stick around and wait for him?

"Go ahead and lay it on us, then," he said, anxious to get back to the ballroom.

Back to Susannah.

The memory of her voice still echoed in his chest. *I love you, Oliver.*

She'd said it with such clarity, such boldness, like she hadn't spent the past year building a wall around her heart. And he hadn't said it back. Not because he didn't feel it—he did, more than he could explain— but because the moment had caught him completely off guard.

Now, with every second that ticked by, he felt the weight of that silence grow heavier. What if she thought his hesitation meant he didn't feel the same? What if she left before he had the chance to say what he should've said the moment she looked at him with those beautiful green eyes?

The lawyer gave a small cough, pulling Oliver back to the present. "As the attorneys for the estate of Archibald Fortune, it is our pleasure to inform you that the terms of the decedent's will have officially been fulfilled. The matter is now closed. The life insurance policy proceeds, along with all other financial assets, have been equally divided among all of you and the money should land in your individual accounts by midnight tonight."

"'The matter is now closed'?" Shelby repeated. "Does that mean..."

"It's finally over," Jillian breathed.

"It is, indeed," the triplet lawyers said in unison.

Creepy, but Oliver didn't even care. This tumultuous time of his life had finally come to a proper end. He was ready to move on.

Really ready.

Not just from the mess Archibald had left behind, but from the version of himself who'd carried so much anger, so many questions and so much fear of not belonging. That part of his story was over now.

Technically, he never had to see the rest of the Fortunes ever again. The estate was settled. The money was wired. The page had been turned.

But deep down, he knew better. They were his family now, and maybe that was the true fortune Archibald had left behind. The real fortune wasn't the land or the money or the legendary name. Instead, it was the strange, unexpected gift of connection and the courage to chase after dreams, even when they seemed impossible.

It would've been so easy for his father to blame his circumstances and never gain the confidence to make his dream of owning an airline come true. Life was full of hardships and heartbreaks. For *everyone*, not just Oliver. It took a special person to overcome their particular fears and put their heart on the line for what they really wanted. That's what Archibald had done all those years ago in Kate Fortune's office.

And that's what Susannah did tonight when she said she wanted a future together.

Oliver wanted to be that kind of person, too.

He straightened his tie, excused himself from the Fortune family gathering and headed for the door. Finding Susannah couldn't wait another second.

He was ready for the next chapter.

* * *

Susannah mingled with the other partygoers for a while after Oliver left with Shelby for the mysterious family meeting, but she couldn't concentrate on a word that anyone said to her. Twice, she'd laughed at the wrong moment, and once she even blurted out an answer to a question that no one had asked her. Her cheeks hurt from smiling, but it was all a show, and now that she'd left Hollywood firmly in her rearview mirror, it seemed as if her acting skills had flown right out the window.

Every time a tall man in a tuxedo drifted into her periphery, her heart stilled. She kept glancing around, searching for Oliver. It was silly, really. Desperate, even. But she just couldn't help it. It wasn't every day that she poured her heart out and told someone she loved them. For all practical purposes, she'd just *proposed* to Oliver mere days after he'd dumped her.

She wasn't even sorry. She liked this new, bold version of herself. The new Susannah followed her heart and reached for her dreams, come what may. She was brave like Nancy Drew...

Even when her Ned Nickerson couldn't quite say that he loved her back.

Susannah drew in a slow breath and straightened her shoulders. Maybe love wasn't always tidy or mutual or timed just right. But even so, she didn't regret saying the words. She'd been hiding for such a long time. She'd never get the past twelve months of her life back. The accident could've *killed* her, and what had she done in the aftermath? Absolutely nothing.

She'd wasted so much precious time.

Tonight, she'd spoken to Oliver from her heart and shared the deepest part of herself, scars and all. No matter what happened next, that had to count for something.

A server balancing a tray of crystal glasses in one of his white-gloved hands paused to bow in front of her. "May I offer you a fresh glass of champagne to enjoy with the fireworks, Miss Simmons?"

Her fingers wrapped around the champagne flute she'd forgotten she was holding. Her drink was warm now…untouched since Oliver had been whisked away. How long had he been gone, exactly?

The memory of his expression still burned in her mind. For a breathless instant, she'd believed he might stay. That the walls between them were finally coming down. But then Shelby had appeared, and in that quiet, careful way of his, he'd stepped back again, retreating before she could see what he truly felt.

"Fireworks?" She blinked. "Is it that time already?"

"Almost. Most of the guests are already making their way outside to watch from the lawn. Or you can watch from the balcony if you prefer." The server took her glass and replaced it with one from his tray. "To toast the night sky."

"Thank you." She gazed down at the bubbles fizzing up to the surface, and when she looked back up, the server was gone and the ballroom empty, save for the string quartet still playing in the corner.

Dismay curled low in her belly as she realized midnight was only minutes away. The party was nearly over. She'd bared her soul to him earlier, and now her confession of love was out there, raw and unanswered, hanging in the air between them. Had Oliver forgotten her promise to wait for him?

What are you still doing here? Are you really going to force him to break your heart twice?

He'd seemed happy to see her, but maybe he was simply being polite. She should go. If Oliver really wanted to talk, they could do it later…in private. Tonight was supposed to be about Kate Fortune, not Susannah and her foolish hopes.

She turned toward the exit, and no sooner did she take a step than she plowed straight into Oliver.

His hands steadied her instantly, warm and sure at her elbows. "Going somewhere?" he asked, his voice low, threaded with something that might've been surprise, or maybe disappointment.

Susannah took a breath, but it didn't steady her. Champagne sloshed at the rim of her glass. "I thought maybe you forgot."

"Not a chance," he said. "I'm sorry it's so late. I didn't mean to be away for so long. There was a lot of family stuff to deal with, but I'm here now and I'm all yours. I promise."

All mine. Could that really be true? It almost felt like too much to hope for after everything they'd both been through.

"The fireworks are about to start. Won't your family be looking for you? Maybe we should go outside with the others." She glanced past him toward the open doors that led to the balcony, where the night pulsed with anticipation and distant bursts of laughter. She put down her glass.

But Oliver didn't move.

"Let them wait," he rasped. "They've had me all night. This…" his gaze locked onto hers, steady and unwavering "…this is the part I've been waiting for."

"It is?" she asked, hope flickering back to life.

"It sure is. I know there's a show going on outside, but I've got a better idea." He arched a brow, and his expression turned boyish. He looked like Oren again—like the person he'd been before the name changes and the betrayals that had chipped away at his youthful innocence.

Hello, old friend. Tears pricked the corners of her eyes, and she knew that whatever the future held for them—whatever came next—*they* would be okay.

"A better idea, huh?" She tilted her head. "Tell me."

"I think we should stay right here and start our own fireworks." He winked, and the gesture seemed to float right through her on butterfly wings. "Dance with me?"

"Are you serious? We're the only people in here." Her laugh was soft, disbelieving, but something warm bloomed in her chest.

Oliver took her hand and pulled her toward the string quartet, where he pressed a few dollars into the violinist's hand.

"Can you play something romantic?" he asked. "Something special, maybe?"

The violinist gave a knowing smile and nodded. A moment later, the first gentle strains of "Waltz across

Texas" filled the air, a classic country love song from the days of Johnny Cash and Patsy Cline.

Oliver pulled her close, until her heartbeat was flush against his. Susannah rested her hand on his shoulder as he guided her into the slow rhythm. Outside, the sky glittered with the first of the fireworks, casting diamond-like shadows over the ballroom floor, and she felt like she might be dreaming.

This felt too good to be real. She'd been holding her breath for such a long time—through her recovery, through the past long, lonely year of wondering if love would ever find her. Even in her best moments, she never thought it would. But here in Oliver's arms, something inside her finally let go. She *believed.*

"I don't want to wake up," she whispered.

"This isn't a dream, sweetheart. This is real." He leaned in and pressed a kiss to her temple.

She tilted her head to look at him, the shimmer of fireworks reflected in his eyes. "Then tell me."

"I love you," he said, without hesitation. "And I'm not going anywhere. Not this time. Not ever."

A sound—half laugh, half sob—escaped her lips as she pressed her forehead to his. "Good, because I love you, too."

"I'm sorry about the things I said before. The truth is, building a life with you here in Emerald Ridge is what I want most in the entire world. Babies and kids included."

Susannah's feet slowed until she was standing completely still. "Seriously?"

"Seriously." He nodded, and this time, it was his

turn to get misty-eyed. "Of course I want a family with you, Susannah. I was just scared before, but Kate Fortune shared some things about Archibald tonight that made me realize that I want to be a better man. *You* make me want to be a better man, sweetheart. So, if you'll have me…"

Oliver took her hand in his and lowered himself to one knee at her feet. Another sob rose up Susannah's throat, and she was vaguely aware of one of the musicians sniffling as the sweet country love song played on.

"Suzy Q, will you marry me?"

"Yes!" Susannah somehow managed to say through her tears. "Now stand up and kiss me, cowboy."

"Always so bossy," Oliver teased as he rose to his feet. He tucked a lock of hair behind her ear. "But I love a woman who knows what she wants and isn't afraid to say it."

Then he cupped her face in his hands and looked at her with a tenderness so sweet that she felt it all the way down to her toes. "I've been waiting to make you my bride since I was fourteen years old. At long last, good fortune has finally found me."

"I think it found us both," Susannah said.

Then she closed her eyes, and when his mouth met hers, the sky overhead bloomed with light. Their love… their good fortune…written in sparks across the wide Texas sky.

Chapter Seventeen

"**M**ads, I thought the fireworks were supposed to be the grand finale." Forrest cast a questioning glance at Madeline, who was nestled against him with his arm slung over her shoulders as the party somehow kicked back into high gear.

Or perhaps this was the after-party? Oliver wasn't sure. All he knew was that he was going to marry the love of his life. Susannah had said yes. That alone was enough reason to party until the wee hours of the morning.

"They were." Madeline scrunched her face.

All six Fortune siblings and their partners had reconvened in the ballroom after the fireworks ended and only half the party guests had left the premises. Oliver's sister had immediately noticed Susannah's hand entwined with his and cast him a dazzling smile, but he and Susannah hadn't shared the news about their engagement yet. For now, it was their little secret.

Call him crazy, but Oliver felt like they should share the happy news with Hershey, Honey and Bear before any humans caught wind of it. When he'd mentioned that to Susannah, she'd given him an affectionate poke in the ribs and called him her favorite "dog dad." Being referred to as a dad—even to a pack of goofball Labradors—had made his chest burst with quiet pride. Tonight, he felt like the luckiest man alive.

"But like I told y'all earlier," Madeline continued, "the party doesn't truly end until Kate Fortune says it ends. Clearly she's not ready to call it a night yet."

"Where is she, anyway?" Shelby's eyes darted around the ballroom.

Around them, party guests had kicked off their shoes. Men danced in their sock feet and women twirled barefoot, stilettos dangling from their fingertips by thin leather straps.

"The last time I saw her, she was on her third piece of birthday cake," Penn said with a grin.

Gia nodded. "Good for her. That cake was well-earned. One hundred years is a long time."

"Oh, she's moved on from cake." Cameron, Shelby's fiancé, waggled his eyebrows. "I saw her at the bar just a few minutes ago drinking whiskey with the triplet lawyers."

Oliver's jaw dropped almost all the way to the floor. Apparently, the grande dame had a change of heart about attorneys. Either that, or she'd decided they were more tolerable with a splash of bourbon.

"To Kate Fortune." Madeline raised her glass. "May we all be so fabulous when we hit the century mark!"

"Hear, hear," Oliver chimed in as he gave Susannah's hand a squeeze and blew her a kiss.

But before he had a chance to toss back his champagne, a booming voice cut through the chatter in the ballroom.

"Nice party. I guess my invitation must've gotten lost in the mail."

The Fortune siblings exchanged wary glances, and then Oliver's gaze zeroed in on the intruder—an eccentric-looking man who looked to be in his late sixties decked out in pricey, ostentatious Western wear. His pearl-snap shirt sparkled with rhinestones under the ballroom lights, and his bolo tie featured a turquoise stone the size of a quail egg. A white Stetson sat atop a head of artfully styled silver hair, and his boots—hand-tooled leather with gleaming silver tips—looked like they'd never touched actual dirt. The man had the air of someone who'd bought a cattle ranch for the aesthetic and promptly hired someone else to run it.

His eyes narrowed under the brim of his hat as he approached the Fortunes.

"Do any of you care to explain why I wasn't on the guest list?" The stranger's lip curled into a sly, devious grin. "I'm a Fortune, after all."

Oliver tightened his grasp on Susannah's hand and gave Madeline a sidelong glance. If this odd gentleman was indeed a Fortune, she should know. She'd spent months rounding up various relatives of Kate from all over the state.

But when their eyes met, all she had to offer was a slow shake of her head.

"What branch?" Oliver cut his gaze back toward the party crasher, squinting against the glare of all those rhinestones.

"Yours, as a matter of fact," he said, eyeing Oliver up and down before shifting his eyes toward the other Fortune siblings, one at a time. "My name is Clemons Fortune. Your father, Archibald, was my older brother by a year."

Someone let out a gasp—Oliver wasn't sure who. In a shaky voice, Jillian told the man their father didn't have a brother.

His response was a deep belly laugh. People around them were starting to stare. "Think again, sweetheart. Our parents gave me up for adoption because they couldn't afford to raise two boys. I've been a family secret all this time. I didn't even realize I was adopted until a few months ago when one of my kids gave me a DNA test as a joke for my birthday."

Oliver wondered if the triplet lawyers were still at the bar. It seemed like their services might be useful in the immediate future.

"I'm sorry to hear about your dear departed father. It's a shame I'll never get the chance to know the brother I never knew existed." Clemons tossed his arms open wide. "But I'm here to welcome myself to the family. I think I'll be quite happy here in Emerald Ridge, and so will my six adult children…even if they aren't exactly on speaking terms with me at the moment. But knowing my kids, they won't be far behind."

He gave an exaggerated wink.

Susannah blinked, stunned into silence, while Oliver merely let out a breath and rubbed a hand down his face.

"Of course he has six children," Hayes muttered. "Why wouldn't he?"

Oliver turned to his beautiful fiancée with a resigned sigh. "Welcome to the Fortunes. Please tell me you still want to marry into this family, drama and all."

She gave his hand a reassuring squeeze, her thumb brushing gently across his knuckles. "I told you I love a little chaos, remember?"

He grinned. "That, you did."

"Mostly, I love *you*." She rose up on tiptoe and kissed his cheek, and Oliver knew that no matter what secrets and scandals lay ahead, he and Susannah had found their happy-ever-after…

Deep in the heart of Emerald Ridge.

* * * * *

Get up to 4 Free Books!

We'll send you 2 free books from each series you try
PLUS a free Mystery Gift.

Both the **Harlequin® Special Edition** and **Harlequin® Heartwarming™** series feature compelling novels filled with stories of love and strength where the bonds of friendship, family and community unite.

YES! Please send me 2 FREE novels from the Harlequin Special Edition or Harlequin Heartwarming series and my FREE Gift (gift is worth about $10 retail). I may cancel anytime by emailing ReaderServiceInfo@Harlequin.com or by calling 1-800-873-8635. If I don't cancel, I will receive 6 brand-new Harlequin Special Edition books every month and be billed just $6.39 each in the U.S. or $7.19 each in Canada, or 4 brand-new Harlequin Heartwarming Larger-Print books every month and be billed just $7.19 each in the U.S. or $7.99 each in Canada, a savings of 20% off the cover price. It's quite a bargain! Shipping and handling is just 75¢ per book in the U.S. and $1.75 per book in Canada.* I understand that accepting the free books and gift places me under no obligation to buy anything—they are mine to keep for free no matter what I decide.

Choose one: ☐ **Harlequin Special Edition**
(235/335 BPA G3CD)

☐ **Harlequin Heartwarming Larger-Print**
(161/361 BPA G3CD)

☐ **Or Try Both!**
(235/335 & 161/361 BPA G3CE)

Name (please print)

Address   Apt. #

City   State/Province   Zip/Postal Code

Email: Please check this box ☐ if you would like to receive newsletters and promotional emails from Harlequin Enterprises ULC and its affiliates. You can unsubscribe anytime.

Mail to the **Harlequin Reader Service:**
IN U.S.A.: P.O. Box 1341, Buffalo, NY 14240-8531
IN CANADA: P.O. Box 603, Fort Erie, Ontario L2A 5X3

Want to explore our other series or interested in ebooks? Visit www.ReaderService.com or call 1-800-873-8635.

HSEHW2603